The Mystery of the Medieval Coin

The Mystery of the Medieval Coin

by A.D. Fast

Vanwell Publishing Limited

St. Catharines, Ontario

Vanwell Publishing acknowledges the financial support of the
Government of Canada through the Book Publishing Industry
Development Program for our publishing activities.

Vanwell Publishing acknowledges the Government of Ontario through
the Ontario Media Development Corporation's Book Initiative.

Vanwell Publishing Limited
P.O. Box 2131
1 Northrup Crescent
St. Catharines, ON
Canada L2R 7S2
sales@vanwell.com
1-800-661-6136

Produced and designed by Tea Leaf Press Inc.
www.tealeafpress.com

Cover illustration: Margaret Amy Reiach

Printed in Canada

National Library of Canada Cataloguing in Publication

Fast, A. D., 1968–
    The mystery of the medieval coin / April Fast.

ISBN 1-55068-127-3

    I. Title.

PS8561.A84M98 2003   C813'.6   C2003-905531-0

To Dana Block, Susan Roberts, Debbie Voth, & Debbie Hunter. Although I wasn't born with sisters, I've been blessed with soul-sisters. Thanks for years of love and laughter. Who would I be without you?

"If he will not listen, then off with his head!" the man shouted, thrusting one arm into the air above his head. His foot was perched on the seat of his chair. His eyes blazed with fury. His long, wavy hair was pulled back from his pale face into a low, untidy ponytail.

"What? Without even a trial?" Marvin asked. Marvin McKnight was in grade five and was not ready to be beheaded. His friends, Lucas and Nicole, stood beside him, their eyes wide and their mouths open. *How could this man accuse me of breaking the law without any proof?* Marvin wondered. *How could he sentence me to death without any trial?*

The man at the front of the classroom lowered his arm and seemed to snap out of the daze he was in. He scratched his short, scruffy beard. The girls in the class giggled. They seemed to find him interesting. Marvin only found him annoying.

Fifth grade was supposed to be awesome, and so much better than grade four. That was until they met their new social studies teacher. Mr. LeClair was new to the school. He had taught the class geography, history, and science all year, and it had been a very long year. Luckily, there were only a few days of school left before summer vacation.

This month, Mr. LeClair had been teaching medieval history. Whenever he taught something new, he would act it out. Like this trial. To many of the students, it was very annoying. He was from France, and his French accent made him hard to understand. Mr. LeClair always boasted about how wonderful his part of the world was.

"This is how things were back then, Marvin," Mr. LeClair said. "If peasants were accused of a crime, they were punished. We did not have to listen to their excuses. I have told you about the feudal system. This system made up the set of rules that people had to live by. If you were a king or a knight, you were at the top. You had all the power. If you were a peasant, you were nothing. And punishment for breaking the laws was the dungeon or death," he added.

"But that's not fair," Lucas spoke up. "Everyone is equal. And everyone is innocent until proven guilty."

Lucas and Marvin sat next to one another in almost every class. It was great for Marvin. He had Lucas close by to stick up for him. It was great for Lucas, too. He had Marvin nearby to help him with his schoolwork. Marvin was the smartest kid at Green Park Elementary School.

"Not in medieval Europe," said Mr. LeClair. "Peasants couldn't even read. How would they know the law? They were so poor that they could not fight those in power. It was wonderful. The rich stayed powerful, and the poor stayed poor. Don't you think it would be better to have such order today?" he asked.

"But—" The bell rang, cutting off Lucas' comment. It was probably a good thing. Lucas didn't like Mr. LeClair.

"For your homework today, I want each student to write a paragraph about how the medieval feudal system was good for people," Mr. LeClair said.

The class groaned. The week before, they had to write a paper on how the invention of the printing press ruined the feudal system. They were supposed to argue that printing books was bad for society. Marvin learned every last thing about the Gutenberg Press. He found out that it was invented around the year 1450 by Johannes Gutenberg, and it was the first machine ever to print words onto paper. The press used ink and metal letters. Books could be printed very quickly after the press was invented. There was no longer any need for scribes, the monks who copied books by hand.

Marvin couldn't find one bad thing about books being printed by a printing press. He almost got a bad grade on the paper. The only thing that saved him was Lucas. Lucas could argue anything, even if it didn't make sense.

The students started to pack up their books and make their way out the door. Mr. LeClair sat down at his desk and opened a book. He was always reading about history.

"He can't be serious," Lucas said. "Does he actually believe that it was a good thing when kings and lords ruled over the poor peasants? Does he actually think that it was a good thing *not* to teach those peasants to read? He is so brutal! We might have him for homeroom next year. That would be even worse!"

Marvin put his pencil and pen into his back pocket. He ran his hand through his short, blond hair. He was about to answer Lucas when Nicole walked over.

"He isn't serious," Nicole said. "He's a teacher! Of course he thinks everyone should learn to read and have equal rights. He is just trying to get us to think about things. He wants us to imagine what life would be like in medieval times. That's all," she said.

They joined the long line of kids that snaked around the back of the class and filed out the door.

Loud voices came from the hallway outside. It was the end of the day. Everyone was in a rush to get to their homeroom. In a few minutes, they would all be free!

"I don't know about that," said Marvin. He looked back at Mr. LeClair. The teacher was engrossed in whatever he was reading. He hardly even looked up from his dusty old book. "I think he almost believes what he says. That guy is weird," he added.

Lucas did his best French accent and rubbed his chin. *"If peasants were accused of a crime, they were punished. We did not have to listen to their excuses,"* he said, imitating Mr. LeClair. "What's all that *we* stuff? I think he reads too much history."

Nicole laughed. "Lucas, he's French, okay? Sometimes things come out a bit different when you are speaking a different language. He just makes a few mistakes, that's all. English is his second language, you know."

"Yes, we know that, thanks. We also know that you're almost as good at French as you are at English. You are the only kid on the planet who likes learning other languages. You always stick up for Mr. LeClair just because he's French," Lucas said jokingly.

"Next time you need help with your French homework, don't come crying to me!" Nicole said.

Marvin was deep in thought as he watched Mr. LeClair ferociously reading the thick books on his desk. There was something very strange about Mr. LeClair. Something more than the fact that he spoke funny. Something more than the way he acted. Something more than the nasty smell that came from his desk. Mr. LeClair was definitely not a regular teacher.

Marvin and Lucas pushed through the busy hallway toward their homeroom. They were in Mrs. Wright's grade five/six split class. Nicole went the other way. She was in another grade five class. When the boys walked into their classroom, Mrs. Wright was sitting at her desk. That was unusual. Mrs. Wright was always standing and always smiling. She was the gym teacher and was very energetic. She had shoulder-length, blond hair that was held back most days by a shiny, gold clip. She was also the only teacher who wore running suits to school. She was young, smart, and very strict. Even though she was a tough teacher, everyone loved her. Mrs. Wright was the best teacher Marvin had ever had.

"Well, good afternoon," Mrs. Wright said. She looked up from the stack of papers on her desk. Then she stood up and walked to the front of the class, her back to the chalkboard. "Please get your books *quietly* from your desks. Don't forget your math homework for tomorrow. Also, we have an author talk in the afternoon, so I expect you all to bring some good questions for her. When you are packed up and waiting silently, I will dismiss you."

She stood smiling at the class while everyone quieted down and rifled through their desks.

"Hey, are you coming rock hounding with us after school?" Marvin asked Lucas. "My grandpa says there are some great rocks out there. He found some stuff yesterday." Marvin's grandfather was an archeologist. He swore that there were diamonds in the rocks by the forest. Marvin and his grandpa went there all the time, and his grandpa had an amazing rock collection. His grandpa also had a collection of things from long ago. He was a history buff and told Marvin all kinds of stories about what life was like hundreds of years ago.

"Sure, I'm game. I wouldn't mind checking out the cave again, too. We should bring bigger flashlights this time. That place is pitch black inside," Lucas said.

"Yeah, we can check it out, but you know how my grandpa feels about it. He says we shouldn't disturb a natural wonder. Besides, he says it might not be safe," Marvin said.

"He thinks it's haunted, that's all!" Lucas said, rolling his eyes. "Besides, we don't have to tell him *every* time we go into the woods. It's our cave. We need to check on it, you know."

Lucas felt very protective of the cave in the woods. They had worked very hard to find it.

Lucas, Marvin, and Marvin's grandpa had cut away trees and moved rocks last year, looking for a certain rock formation. That was when they had stumbled upon the small cave. They had heard about the cave—everyone in town knew that there was a hidden cave somewhere in the woods—but they had never expected to find it. They found no diamonds or precious rocks, of course. Just one very cool cave. They had kept it hidden—and secret—ever since. Nicole was the only other person they had told about it.

"Boys," Mrs. Wright called from the front of the class. "Why are you the only ones talking?" Marvin looked around. Everyone else was sitting quietly with their books on their desks. They were all staring at Lucas and Marvin.

"Sorry, Mrs. Wright," Marvin said. He hoped no one had heard them talking about the cave. He didn't want anyone else finding it. It was too cool to have to share. He also hated getting in trouble.

"Sorry, Mrs. Wright," Lucas said, smiling. "That was very rude of us." He had bright blue eyes and short, red hair spiked up in the front with blond tips.

No teacher could stay mad at Lucas. Lucas had a way of making adults laugh. Mrs. Wright always laughed at Lucas.

Mrs. Wright stepped toward the desks where Lucas and Marvin sat. She made a *tsk* sound with her teeth. "Lucas Maxwell, you are something else," she said, laughing. "Okay, class. Now that everyone is silent, you may be dismissed. Have a terrific day!" she said.

The boys put their books into their backpacks and left the classroom. As they walked down the hall, they passed Mr. LeClair's room. Marvin glanced into the room as he passed, and he stopped in his tracks. Lying on Mr. LeClair's desk was a shiny, silver knife. It had a green stone set into the handle. It was lying beside a brown leather pouch. Mr. LeClair was sitting at his desk reading a book. He pounded the desk angrily with his fist. Then he ran his hand through his hair and said something to himself. Suddenly, he looked up from his desk and turned toward the classroom door. His icy green eyes bored into Marvin like two laser beams. He quickly slid the knife into a drawer.

Marvin looked away and started walking quickly down the hall to catch up with Lucas. *Why would Mr. LeClair have a knife on his desk? That's not good. A crazy person with a sharp knife. I wish he hadn't seen me*, Marvin thought. He had an uneasy feeling in his stomach.

Nicole was waiting for them at the side door of the school. She pushed open the heavy door and sunlight streamed into the hallway. Marvin squinted against the bright sunshine and took a deep breath of the grass-scented air. The summer air was warm, and it felt good after a long day inside. There were only a few more days until summer holidays began.

They walked across the parking lot to the soccer field behind it. The parking lot was filled with cars, and parents were everywhere, calling for their kids. Marvin was so glad he wasn't one of those kids anymore.

"So, who's coming to the cave?" Lucas asked as they strolled past the cars and onto the freshly cut grass of the soccer field. He looked over at

Nicole, who was concentrating on her white running shoes. She was trying to make sure they didn't get dirty.

"Hello? Anybody home?" Lucas said.

Nicole still didn't answer.

"Looks like those new shoes of yours are bothering you. How about I help you dirty them up so they aren't so distracting?" Lucas stepped toward Nicole, pretending to step on her shoe.

"Get lost!" she shrieked, running toward the path up ahead. Her long brown ponytail bounced as she ran.

"Nice sparkly, boppy things in your hair, Nicole. And I see you have pink nail polish on, too. You went out with your aunt again, didn't you?"

"Yes, it was our annual shopping trip, thank you very much. I would like to at least look decent for a few days. How come you notice every little tiny thing about people?" Nicole asked. She had stopped by the fence to wait for the boys.

"I'm a details person," Lucas answered. He put his baseball cap on backward and pulled his sunglasses out of his backpack.

"Sure, except when it comes to school," Marvin called from behind.

"Ouch. That one hurt, Marvin. That really hurt," Lucas said, pretending to be upset.

"Get lost," Marvin said, laughing. He caught up to Lucas and Nicole. "Seriously, I'm game to go to the cave. I don't have to be home until five."

"Me neither," Nicole added.

They walked down the path that cut from the soccer field to the neighborhood. A few streets later, they reached Marvin's house. It was at the end of the street, near the forest. Marvin ran up to his garage with all three backpacks and dumped them on the ground. Then he ran back to the road where Lucas and Nicole were waiting.

"Okay, let's go!" Marvin said. He was always happier when he was exploring in the woods. Everyone told him he was just like his grandpa. He had a knack for discovering things.

The forest was at the end of Marvin's street. There were no marked paths and no picnic areas. Few people actually went into the woods—and Marvin would know. He had grown up on the dead-end street and spent plenty of time in the forest. He could also see the entrance to the forest from his bedroom window.

Inside the forest, it was dark and cool. Sunlight tried to peek through the leaves of the trees, but only bits of light made it through the thick canopy of branches overhead. Jagged patches of light lay on the ground below like sparkling pieces of shattered glass. The minute the three friends walked into the woods, they felt like they had walked into another world. Suddenly, the noise of cars and people faded away into the distance. Instead, they could hear birds and crickets chirping and frogs croaking in the pond past the hill. Sticks crackled under their feet, and bugs flew around in front of them like tiny torpedoes.

"The woods are lovely, dark and deep. But I have promises to keep. And miles to go before I sleep. And miles to go before I sleep. That's by Robert Frost. Famous poet," Nicole announced as she walked through the woods.

"You're brutal," Lucas said. "You really have to stop reading so much poetry. I may have to stop hanging out with you."

Nicole reached back and slapped him on the arm. "Sure. You could always hang out with your *millions* of other friends."

"Hey, I'm a likeable guy, you know," Lucas said. He rubbed his arm, pretending to be hurt.

The cave was at the other end of the huge forest. The farther they walked, the thicker the woods got. On the left was a rocky ridge where Marvin's grandpa liked to go rock hounding. His grandpa usually brought a whole kit with him, including a magnifying glass, picks, and an eyepiece to examine the rocks. Today, they weren't stopping for rocks. They were going straight to the cave.

Lucas, Marvin, and Nicole walked almost a mile before they came to the "little hills." That was their name for the small hills that lined the far edge of the forest. Beyond the little hills was the escarpment, a huge rocky ridge. It felt like being at the end of the earth.

Nicole reached down and slapped her leg. "Ow! Take that, bug," she said. Nicole loved to catch, squash, or just inspect bugs. This time, she was out for blood. She straightened up and stopped in her tracks. Lucas and Marvin were standing frozen in front of the cave. They were both staring at it, mouths open. Neither of them moved.

Someone had been in the cave.

The three friends were careful to cover up the opening to the cave every time they left. They propped up long tree branches across the opening and even rolled a few small boulders in front of it. The cave was barely visible when they were done covering it up. Now the branches and rocks were gone, and the cave was completely exposed.

"No way," Marvin said. "Nobody else knows about it. It must have been an animal."

"Sure, Marvin. Those squirrels are good with their hands. They probably stood up, pushed aside the branches, moved the rocks, and went inside," Lucas said.

"It's not a big deal," Nicole said as she brushed past the boys to peer into the dark cave. "Maybe someone found it. It's just a cave. We can't be the only ones in the world who know about it. Remember what your grandpa said? About fifty years ago someone figured out what the symbols on the wall meant."

"*Midnight fly, by twenty-four, back in time no time shall pass. Miss the door in twenty-four and no more,*" Marvin said. "I know. I have been trying to figure that out since I was a little kid. Whoever interpreted that carving was full of it. It doesn't even make sense. But I'm telling you, that cave has been undisturbed for a long time! Remember what we had to go through to get to the opening? And if anyone had been in the forest, I would know about it. Unless…" Marvin stopped. He was puzzled. "Unless it was the person I keep seeing going into the forest late at night."

"Marvin, that was probably just some poor slob out for a walk on your street who wasn't even going into the forest, let alone the cave," Lucas said. He bit his nails for a minute, looking concerned. "What if another group of stupid kids found it?"

"What, like us stupid kids?" Nicole answered.

"No, I mean…you know what I mean, Nic. What if some other kids have found it and are going to make it *their* secret cave?" Lucas said.

"It would be worse if some stupid adult found it. They would either want to show all their friends or would want to bring their stupid kids," Marvin said. He was not happy. "What if a gang found it? What if a criminal is hiding out in there now?" Marvin asked.

"What if some hiker found it, said '*cool*,' and then moved on?" Nicole answered, making a face at Marvin. "I'm sure that whoever found it has forgotten about it by now. If it'll make you feel better, let's go in and make sure no one has moved in any furniture."

They stepped into the cave opening and stopped to listen. Lucas had to duck to go inside. No sounds came from the back of the cave. Marvin grabbed his flashlight, which hung from a key chain on his belt loop. "Not cool, but very useful," he always said.

The thin beam of light cut through the darkness of the cave. The front part of the cave was low and narrow. The walls were rocky and dirty. Once they walked inside a few steps, the cave opened up and was quite big.

"See? It doesn't look like anyone has been here. At least whoever it was didn't stay very long. I don't see any garbage or anything," Nicole said. "Hey, wait. What's that?" She pointed to something on the ground.

Marvin walked over to the small gum wrapper on the ground and picked it up to look at it. He knew that wrapper well. It was the same gum his grandpa chewed all the time.

"Well, well, well," Nicole said, smiling. "Who do we know that keeps Ultra Fresh Mint gum in his pocket all the time?"

Marvin didn't say anything for a moment. Then he shook his head. "No, he wouldn't come in here without telling us. He never comes into the cave anymore."

"Not that you know of," Lucas said. "Maybe he has taken a sudden interest in the carving again. Maybe he's the one you've seen going into the forest at night."

Marvin shone the light up at the far right-hand wall. At the end of the wall was their big find—a carving that looked like some kind of ancient language. It was a message, but they couldn't read it, of course. Some archeologist had studied it about fifty years ago and translated it into English. It had been big news back then, even though no one understood what the message meant. But over the years, the people in town forgot about it. The cave receded back into the branches and rocks that kept it hidden and the translated message was dismissed as folklore or nonsense.

"No, it couldn't have been my grandpa. He would have told me," Marvin said. "Good thing nobody ruined this carving. We should cover it up. If it got covered in paint or something, that would be terrible."

"Yes, I know some home decorators who would love to come in here, slap on some paint, and call it home," Lucas said sarcastically.

"You know what I mean. What if it got covered in graffiti or something?" Marvin said. "We have to be extra careful now that someone else knows about the cave." He walked closer to the carving. It was etched into the wall just above his eye level. He reached up to touch it with his finger.

"Something is up with this carving," he said, staring at the designs etched into the stone wall. "I wish I could figure out what this *really* means."

"It was probably done by someone thousands of years ago. Maybe Vikings," Lucas said.

"Hello? Vikings didn't settle this part of North America. They were in Newfoundland, genius. And it was not thousands of years ago, it was hundreds of years ago. Anyway, you're right about one thing. This is a message from hundreds of years ago. It is trying to tell us something," Marvin said. "This is something…" He didn't finish his sentence.

"Something special, right?" Lucas said. He was sitting on his "chair." It was a large rock by the wall of the cave. "You get that look whenever you find a little stone or rock that looks different. You and your grandpa think it's *special*."

Marvin ran his hand over the carving again. "Whatever. But there is a story here. I can guarantee it." He didn't say anything to the others, but he did feel something. Whenever he ran his fingers over the carving, they tingled. One day he was going to find out what it meant.

When Marvin left the cave, he couldn't help but wonder who had been in it. He thought about it all the way back to his house. Lucas and Nicole picked up their backpacks and went home to eat dinner. When Marvin went inside, his mom and dad were in the kitchen, setting the table.

His mom was home early from the local community theater. She volunteered in the productions and acted in most of the plays. Tonight she was wearing her silver crown. *She must have finished cleaning the house,* Marvin thought to himself. Every time she cleaned the house, she wore her tiara. She said it reminded her that she was the queen of the house.

Marvin's dad was still wearing his shirt and tie. He was an engineer at a chemical plant in town.

He was tall and good-looking, and he had the same short, blond hair that Marvin had.

"Well hello there! Where did you and your friends go off to after school? Don't tell me. You were in the forest, right?" Marvin's mom said, stirring a pot on the stove.

Marvin smiled when he realized that the spicy, rich smell in the air was his mother's famous spaghetti sauce. "Ha ha. You know we always go there," he answered, sitting down at the table.

"Did you find anything awesome?" his dad asked, trying to imitate the way Marvin and his friends talked. "Did anything freak you out?"

"No, nothing *awesome*. We were just hanging out," Marvin said. He tried to keep a straight face. His dad always did that—he acted like he was young and cool even though he knew that it embarrassed Marvin. He told the same jokes, and he always asked the same questions. Marvin tried to convince his father that his jokes weren't funny anymore, even if they were.

"Oh. That's too bad. I bet you wish you had come home to do your homework," his father said, smiling a little bit. He poured a glass of iced tea and sat down in a chair.

Marvin rolled his eyes. "I do my homework after dinner, remember?"

"Well, that could be a problem tonight. I ran over your backpack in the garage by accident," his father said.

"James, do you ever stop teasing him?" Marvin's mom called from the stove. She brought a pot to the table and filled their plates. Big meatballs sat on top of spaghetti, all covered with cheese.

After dinner was finished, Marvin put the dishes in the dishwasher and went to his room. He sat at his desk, pulled out his math homework, and grabbed his pencil from his back pocket.

He couldn't seem to focus on the questions, though. All evening he kept thinking about the cave, and it didn't help that his telescope peered at him from the corner of the room. Marvin's grandpa had bought him the telescope to study the stars. He told Marvin that he believed that not only were there other worlds out there, but probably other living beings, too. Marvin wasn't sure he believed his grandpa's theories, but it was fun looking for new galaxies among the stars.

Marvin couldn't resist any longer. He put down his pencil and grabbed the cool, silver telescope. He moved it into position by the window. He wasn't going to look for stars tonight. He was planning to check out the entrance to the forest.

Marvin stared out into the eerie darkness for quite a while, at times focusing on trees near the edge of the forest. He was hoping to catch a glimpse of the late-night hiker that he had seen for the past few nights. But no one appeared. Finally, he turned the telescope to the sky and scanned the darkness for bright dots of light. He found stars to be very interesting, but he also loved looking at the moon. *It really does look like a ball of Swiss cheese,* he thought.

Before he knew it, it was very late. He turned the telescope back to the entrance to the forest one last time. Still nothing. Then he squeezed his tired eyes shut, opened them wide again, and decided to return to his math homework.

Just as he was about to put his telescope back, he saw something move in the darkness. It didn't take long to realize that it was actually *someone.* Marvin peered through his telescope and tried to focus on the dark figure moving down the street. The person was headed straight for the forest, and seemed to be looking over one shoulder. Marvin couldn't focus very well on the person's face, but at least he was getting a closer view than ever before. This was the seventh night in a row that Marvin had seen someone sneaking into the forest late at night. He checked his watch. *Just before midnight again,* he thought. *Hmm.*

Any other time he had seen the person walking toward the forest, Marvin had simply been looking out his window into the sleeping neighborhood. He hadn't been able to tell who it was, or whether it was a man or a woman. This time, at least, he had his telescope out.

Marvin stared at the blurry shape as it walked to the dead end of the street, looked around, and then switched on a flashlight and headed into the forest. Marvin fumbled with the lens of his telescope, and the figure came into focus. He got a clear view just as the person disappeared into the trees. His mouth dropped open. His heart was pounding. He instantly recognized the blue jacket going into the woods.

Marvin put his telescope down and grabbed the black phone that sat on his desk. His hands were shaking as he dialed.

Lucas picked up after the first ring. "Hello?" he said in a groggy voice.

"I know who it is," Marvin said.

"What?" Lucas asked. "It's almost midnight, man. What are you talking about?"

"I saw someone going into the forest again tonight, for about the millionth time in a row," Marvin answered. He was almost out of breath.

"That's your big news? That you saw someone go into the forest?" Lucas said.

"Yeah, but listen to this. I can't believe I didn't think of it before. Every night for the past week, I've seen someone going into the forest just before midnight, but I couldn't see who it was. Actually, I didn't really care all that much—until I found out that someone else had found our cave. Anyway, I wanted to see who the person was. You know, what if it is the same person who found the cave?" Marvin said.

"Yeah, so..." Lucas said.

"So, this time I *saw* the person. And I know who it is," Marvin whispered. He thought he heard his dad coming down the hall. Marvin was not allowed on the phone so late at night. He was supposed to be in bed hours ago.

"No way," Lucas said. "How could you tell who it was?"

"Telescope," Marvin answered.

"Well? Come on, man! Who is it? And how do you know the person found our cave? I mean, you can't see all the way to the cave from your room," Lucas said.

"It's Mr. LeClair," Marvin said.

There was dead silence.

"Get...OUT!" Lucas whispered loudly.

"No, I'm not getting out. I'm totally serious. Mr. Freaky-Social-Studies-LeClair is going into the forest at night and lurking around our cave! And he didn't look like he was just going for a late-night hike. He looked up and down the street first, like he was hiding something," Marvin said, talking as quietly as he could.

"What the heck would he be doing in the cave?" Lucas asked.

"Uh, think about it. He is a history nut. He's probably trying to figure out what that carving means, just like us. I bet he knows something about that cave. I told you it was special," Marvin said.

"Are you going to call Nicole and tell her?" Lucas asked.

"Are you kidding? Her dad likes me, but if I called this late he'd have my head. She doesn't have her own line like you do. No way. We'll have to tell her tomorrow," Marvin said.

When they said good-bye, Marvin hung up the phone and turned out his lamp. The moon cast a dim, ghostly light into the dark room. He crawled under his puffy, blue-and-green striped blanket and stared at the ceiling. He tried to fall asleep, but he could only think of one thing.

When Marvin and Lucas got to school the next day, they looked everywhere for Nicole. She never met up with them to walk to school. She took too long to get ready in the morning. Also, she usually forgot her lunch and had to run back home. Instead, they had a meeting spot around the back of the school, near the metal climbers.

The schoolyard was packed when Marvin and Lucas arrived. Some kids were playing basketball, and others were just hanging around in small groups. Mrs. Wright was on yard duty. Lucas went over to say hello to her and then joined Marvin by the climbers.

Nicole ran over a few minutes before the bell rang. Her hair was still wet. She stopped and leaned on the climber.

"What happened to you?" Marvin asked. "You're late, and you're still not ready!"

"I know. First of all, I slept in. Then, I forgot my gym shoes. I had to run back or I'd get in trouble from Mrs. Wright. She hates it when I forget my stuff," Nicole answered, rolling her eyes. She was still panting. She bent over and put her hands on her knees, trying to catch her breath.

"Hey, I saw someone going into the woods last night, just before midnight. I had my telescope out, so I got a good look," Marvin said. He looked around to make sure no one could hear him.

"Oh really? Who was it?" Nicole asked.

"Get this—it was Mr. LeClair! And he was looking around the neighborhood before he went in. It looked suspicious to me. Plus, I've seen a person going into the forest every night for a week," Marvin said.

"What were you doing spying into the woods with your telescope at midnight?" Nicole asked.

"I'm always up late, but last night I was watching to see if anyone was going into the forest. We want to know who found our cave, don't we?" Marvin asked.

"No, *you* want to find out who found our cave," Nicole answered.

"Come on. You're wondering, too. Admit it!" Marvin said.

"Well, there is no way Mr. LeClair is going into the forest every night at midnight. Besides, he wouldn't be interested in some dumb old cave. You just can't leave him alone, can you?" said Nicole. "Did you actually see his face?"

Marvin stared at her for a second. "Well, no. I saw his jacket. He wears a blue jacket. You know the one," he answered.

"His jacket? That's all you saw?" Nicole asked. She laughed a bit, and then she sighed. "Marvin, that could have been anyone."

"Yeah, your grandpa has a blue jacket. It could have been him," Lucas said.

Marvin thought about that for a minute. "No way. He wouldn't be going into the forest late at night without me, would he?"

Nicole shrugged. "Who knows? He has all kinds of projects and discoveries going on. If he thinks he found something valuable out there, he would go out at night, making sure no one saw him. Remember when he sneaked around in the forest when he thought he had discovered sapphires?"

"Hey you guys, I had a thought. Listen to this. Since we want to know who is going into the woods at night, and if this person found the cave, let's see for ourselves. What if we go camping in the woods tonight? We can set up our tents near the little hills and see if anyone comes in the middle of the night," Lucas said, grinning.

"By ourselves? Are you nuts? My parents won't let me go camping in the woods alone. We would need an adult there," Nicole said.

Lucas smiled. "Well, I know someone who would do it."

"Who?" Marvin asked.

"Your grandpa! Let's get him to take us camping out in the woods tonight. He'd do it. Besides, he might need a good excuse to get out there at night anyway. I mean, if he's the one going out there every night, he would want to do it for sure," said Lucas.

Marvin smiled. "That's a great idea. Do you think you would be allowed?"

Both Lucas and Nicole shrugged. Seconds later, the school bell rang. As they walked to the door, Marvin saw Mr. LeClair and felt the teacher staring at him. He turned to Lucas and Nicole. "Hey, I forgot to tell you guys something else," he whispered. "Yesterday after school, I saw Mr. LeClair in his classroom, looking at some books. Guess what he had on his desk?"

"Um, books?" Nicole guessed. They filed into the school with the rest of the kids. The halls were noisy with the sounds of voices.

"Um, no!" Marvin answered. "A knife."

"What do you mean? He had a butter knife?" she asked.

"Yeah, that's what I found so interesting. I was completely freaked out by a butter knife," he said sarcastically. "No, Nicole, he had a sharp knife on his desk. Like a dagger. I saw it as plain as day. It even had a jewel on the silver handle. I would recognize it anywhere. And he saw me watching him!" Marvin said.

"That's brutal," Lucas said. "I wonder if it's still there."

"Maybe he keeps it in his desk," Marvin said.

"No way. Even if he did have a knife, he would have taken it home. Teachers don't leave stuff like that in their desks," Nicole said. She was about to turn down the hall to go to her homeroom.

"There's only one way to find out," Lucas said, smiling. "Meet you at lunch time?"

Nicole smiled and shook her head. "No way, Lucas. I'm not digging around in a teacher's desk. Forget it," she said. "You guys just don't like him. He is not some crazy person with a knife in his desk who lurks around in the forest at night. Get a grip."

"Maybe he is. Listen, all you have to do is keep him busy long enough for *us* to do it," Lucas told her.

Nicole didn't say yes or no. She just glared at Lucas, ducked down the hall, and was gone.

The boys put their backpacks in their lockers outside Mrs. Wright's classroom and then walked into the room and sat down at their desks.

"If you're serious, I'm in," Marvin said. "I think we need to know if he keeps a knife in there. That's not safe for anybody. Besides, I don't care what Nicole says. He's weird. And a weird guy with a knife is dangerous. We could all be in trouble. I think he has it in for me."

Lucas laughed. "No kidding. We aren't his favorite students, that's for sure. If he does have a weapon in his desk, though, he could get fired! That would be so awesome! I really don't want him as a teacher next year. I also really don't want some psycho with a knife teaching me social studies. We need to find that knife."

"What are we going to do? He spends all his time in there reading history books," Marvin said.

"We just need Nicole to get him out of the classroom for a few minutes. Then we can look around a bit," Lucas answered thoughtfully.

Marvin smiled. "That's it! Nicole can ask him to help her find a book about medieval France. He'll eat that up! He'll go and help her in the library."

Everyone was supposed to stand for the national anthem. Lucas and Marvin slowly stood up. The rest of the class was already standing.

"He won't want to help a kid with anything," Lucas said. "Not even with a history book. No, we need something that he *really* cares about."

They finished listening to the national anthem and sat down. Mrs. Wright told them to get out their math books and hand in their homework.

"I've got it!" Lucas said.

Mrs. Wright looked over at Lucas from the front of the class. "That's great, Lucas. Just pass it forward with the others, please," she said.

Lucas looked embarrassed. He leaned over to Marvin. "I meant I've got the plan. Nicole can tell

Mr. LeClair that she heard some kids talking about snooping through his desk, which is true. Then she can say that she thinks they went out near the soccer field. He'll get angry and follow her outside. Then we can go in," he whispered.

Marvin nodded his head slowly, a small smile spreading across his face. He figured the plan would work. All they had to do was wait for lunch. And hope like crazy that they didn't get caught.

Marvin watched the clock tick slowly. It seemed to take forever to get from eleven-thirty to noon. With each passing minute, his heart pounded harder. *Should we do it?* he wondered. *If we get caught, will we be expelled? Worse, will it give Mr. LeClair a reason to use his knife?* Marvin decided that it had to be done, no matter how risky it was. The safety of the school depended on it. If Mr. LeClair was a weirdo, they had to find out. They had to get rid of him.

When the bell finally rang, Lucas and Marvin looked at each other. "Show time," Lucas said. He nodded his head.

They had gone over the plan quickly at recess. Nicole didn't want to do it, but she finally agreed. She said they wouldn't find anything anyway. And she knew if the boys were determined to go through Mr. LeClair's desk, someone had to keep Mr. LeClair out of the way.

The class filed out of the room. The only thing louder than the voices in the hall was the beating of Marvin's heart. He was nervous. Nicole was waiting at the fountain down the hallway. She kept looking over her shoulder. She didn't want Mr. LeClair to come out and see her talking to the boys.

"This is Flying Eagle to Drowned Rabbit, do you copy?" Lucas said into his cupped hands as they approached Nicole.

"Shhhh. What is wrong with you? This is supposed to be quiet and serious, not loud and stupid. Oh yeah, *you* are involved," she whispered.

"I take offense to that," Lucas said.

"Can you guys stop it? Nicole, you are going to get Mr. LeClair out into the schoolyard for at least ten minutes, right?" Marvin said. He wiped his sweaty palms on his shorts.

"Yes, I'll keep him away for ten minutes. Just hurry up, and don't mess up his stuff. If he finds out someone was really in there, I'll be in trouble, too," she said.

"Nic, have you seen the man's desk? It's messier than his hair," Lucas said.

"Whatever. Just don't leave any sign that you were in his desk," she said. "By the way, I hate you for this."

"Ah, how sweet of you to say," Lucas said.

Nicole went into Mr. LeClair's classroom. The boys took off down the hall to wait until she and Mr. LeClair left. They pressed themselves flat against the wall. After a few minutes, they could hear Nicole talking to Mr. LeClair in the hallway. Their voices got farther away, and then they disappeared out the door. They were gone.

Marvin looked at his watch. It was 12:07. They had exactly ten minutes.

Quietly, Marvin and Lucas walked toward Mr. LeClair's classroom. The door was open just a crack. That was good. No one would be able to see them snooping around.

They sneaked through the narrow opening of the door. They didn't want to open it all the way in case Nicole and Mr. LeClair came back.

Maps covered every inch of the walls. History facts were written all over the blackboard. Lucas made a beeline between the rows of desks to Mr. LeClair's desk, and Marvin followed.

They stopped in front of the desk. Books, note pads and notebooks littered the top of it. They were covered in Mr. LeClair's sloppy handwriting, but the boys couldn't read it. It was all in French. They looked around the room one more time. Once they were sure nobody was coming, they went for the top drawer.

Slowly, Marvin slid open the wooden drawer. Pens, paper, folders, paper clips. Nothing unusual. They moved a few things but found nothing.

The next few drawers were the same. Files and papers were in the bottom left-hand drawer. The bottom right-hand drawer held books, some erasers and rulers, and a long black box. Marvin was confused. There was no knife in sight.

He looked at Lucas and shrugged his shoulders. "I know he had it," Marvin whispered. He looked at the large, rectangular, black box. *The knife might fit in there,* he thought. He bent over and slowly opened the black box. Scraps of paper and three shiny gold coins lay inside it. The coins looked interesting. They were not from North America, that was for sure. Marvin reached in and picked up a coin. He was looking at the odd design when he heard voices.

It was Nicole and Mr. LeClair.

Lucas' eyes widened in fear.

Marvin looked at his watch. It said 12:11. It had not even been five minutes yet! He started to panic. "We've got to get out of here!" he whispered, looking around for an escape.

"...but Mr. LeClair, why don't we look around outside some more," Nicole's panicked voice carried into the classroom from the hallway.

Marvin knew they were running out of time. He shut the black box and quickly slid the desk drawer closed. Sweat was forming on his forehead. He didn't know what to do. They couldn't hide in the classroom or they would be stuck in there all afternoon. Sooner or later, they would get caught.

Suddenly Marvin felt a sharp pain in his side. Lucas had elbowed him. Marvin gave him a nasty look, but then he smiled with relief. Lucas was pointing to an open window right beside the desk.

"Well, let me get the door for you, sir," Marvin could hear Nicole say. "I'm sure no one is in there right now!" Nicole and Mr. LeClair seemed to be just outside the door. Nicole was speaking loudly, obviously trying to warn the boys that she and the teacher were coming.

They had no time to waste. Lucas hurried to the window. He stuck out his head and wiggled through the opening. He fell with a thud to the ground below.

Marvin was right behind him. He hung out the window and tried to pull his legs after him. He dropped to the ground like a sack of rocks and landed on top of Lucas. They could hear the teacher and Nicole talking back in the classroom. Nicole sounded relieved. Mr. LeClair sounded annoyed.

Marvin rolled to the side and lay still on the ground. He and Lucas stayed there for a moment, stones and twigs jabbing them everywhere. Slowly, they crept along the ground on their stomachs until they were sure they were far from Mr. LeClair's classroom. Then they hopped to their feet and ran around to the back of the school.

Lucas started to laugh. "That was close. We could have been so busted," he said. "At least we know that he doesn't keep a knife in his desk."

Marvin didn't answer. He was staring at something in his hand. Lucas walked over to take a look. Marvin was holding a gold coin.

"No way. You stole Mr. LeClair's money?" Lucas asked. "Are you completely crazy?"

"I didn't mean to take it. I just forgot to put it back in the black box," Marvin answered. "Look at it. He must collect stuff from medieval times. I think I just took a piece of his coin collection."

Lucas squinted his eyes and took a closer look at the coin.

Marvin turned the coin over in his hand a few times. He thought it looked like a penny that had been run over by a train. It was not a perfect circle. It had a picture of a king and the words "Charles VII" stamped onto it. There were other words, too, but the boys couldn't understand them. The coin sparkled in the sunlight. Marvin's hand was shaking slightly.

"Remember we learned that King Charles VII ruled France from 1422 to 1461? That means this coin must be from the 1400s," Marvin said slowly. "And Mr. LeClair had three of them."

"Wow. This is probably worth a lot of money, anyway. What are you going to do with it?" Lucas asked him.

"I don't know. I guess I'll have to put it back," Marvin said. "I can't keep it."

"What do you mean, *put it back?* That is way too risky. We were lucky we didn't get caught just now," Lucas said. He had his hands on his hips. His eyebrows were scrunched up.

"Well, we'll have to go back in there one of these days and put the coin back in the black box. If this is part of a collection, he'll miss it for sure. And like you said, it is probably worth a lot of money. My grandpa has coins from the 1800s, but he doesn't have anything like this," Marvin said. He took one last look at the coin. Then he closed his fist and put it in his pocket.

Lucas and Marvin hung out at the back of the soccer field for the rest of the lunch period. Nicole finally came outside, but she stayed away from the two boys. Marvin knew she was worried that Mr. LeClair might be suspicious if he saw them talking. When they went inside for afternoon classes, they didn't go past Mr. LeClair's room.

Marvin was disappointed that he hadn't found the evidence he needed to prove Mr. LeClair was a weirdo. The coin collection was very cool, but it didn't exactly make Mr. LeClair a dangerous psychopath.

The bell rang at the end of last class, and the whole room jumped up. Everyone was happy to hear that bell, especially on Fridays.

Marvin and Lucas met Nicole inside the front doors of the school. "Hey, what happened to you guys?" Nicole whispered. "When Mr. LeClair and I were walking into that classroom, I was freaking out! I thought he was going to catch you for sure."

"The window," Lucas said, smiling proudly.

"You guys are so lucky that Mr. LeClair didn't catch you going through his desk," she said. "He was totally not happy with me for dragging him away. When we got back to the classroom, I had to stand there for at least twenty minutes listening to him talk about medieval times. So…did you find the knife?"

"No," Marvin answered.

Nicole shook her head and smirked. "Ha. I knew it."

"Show her what you stole," Lucas said.

Marvin jabbed him with his elbow. "Shut up! I didn't steal it. I took it by accident," Marvin whispered. He looked around the hallway to make sure no one heard him, and then he reached into his pocket and took out the gold coin.

"You took his money?" Nicole asked. Her eyes were wide.

"No, it's not regular money. Look at it," Marvin said. "It must be part of his coin collection. He actually collects stuff from the 1400s. This is a medieval coin."

"So what if he collects medieval stuff? He loves that time period. You collect rocks. Nobody thinks *you're* a weirdo," Nicole said.

"I do," Lucas said quickly. He never missed a chance to make a joke.

"You can't keep that coin, you know, Marvin," Nicole added.

Suddenly, a bloodcurdling cry filled the hallway. Marvin, Lucas, and Nicole looked at one another in shock. It sounded like a man screaming in pain, and it was coming from the direction of Mr. LeClair's classroom.

"What was that?" Nicole gasped, looking over her shoulder.

Marvin and Lucas exchanged guilty looks. "Um, it sounds like Mr. LeClair is a little bit upset," Lucas said.

"Oh no," Marvin groaned. "I bet he just noticed that the coin is missing. He must be going crazy in there! Let's get the heck out of here!"

They practically ran out the front doors of the school to the street outside.

"I know I can't keep it, Nic," Marvin said. He put the coin back into his pocket. "I just have to wait until I can put it back."

"Okay, but you're on your own this time. You should leave Mr. LeClair alone. He's just a little different, that's all," Nicole said.

"A little different? Come on..." Marvin started to say.

"Forget about that for a minute. Are we going to camp out in the woods tonight or what?" Lucas said. "I'm going to have to know now. I need to tell my parents before they go out for dinner or I won't be allowed to go. My aunt is supposed to come over to, um, hang out."

"You mean baby-sit?" Nicole said.

"Whatever," Lucas snapped. His parents still wouldn't let him stay home alone.

"You do realize one thing—if my grandpa takes us camping, we have to go rock hounding. And you will both have to be very interested. Get it?" Marvin said.

Nicole and Lucas looked at one another. Marvin knew they weren't as interested in rocks and history as he and his grandpa. But they also thought Marvin's grandpa was really cool, even if he did have some crazy ideas.

"That's fine with me, Marvin. I can look at rocks for a while," Nicole said. "Your grandpa is funny. This will be great! Besides, then you will finally find out what Mr. LeClair is doing. Maybe then you'll stop being so paranoid!"

"Yeah, that's okay," Lucas said. "It's our only way into the woods at night without sneaking out. And it will be fun. I love camping. It's the only time I get to eat junk food! Besides, I like Dave. He's like a young guy in an old guy's body."

Marvin's grandpa liked all the kids to call him Dave. He was outgoing and fun, and full of energy. Even though Marvin's friends called his parents "Mr. and Mrs. McKnight," they called his grandpa just plain "Dave."

As soon as he got home, Marvin called his grandpa to ask him about camping out. It was last minute, but his grandpa was happy to do it. Besides, it was only one night and only a mile from his house.

Lucas, Marvin, and Nicole walked down the street with armloads of camping stuff. Marvin's grandpa met them at the entrance to the forest and helped carry a few sleeping bags. Dave didn't have anything of his own to carry. After Marvin called him, he had gone straight to the woods to set up his tent and lay out his sleeping bag.

When they got near the little hills, Marvin could see two tents through the trees. Dave had set up one tent for himself and one for the boys. Nicole was bringing a small tent for herself. The tents were exactly where the boys wanted them. Marvin had told his grandpa that they wanted to camp close to the cave. His grandpa thought the kids were trying to spook themselves.

Marvin didn't want to mention anything about Mr. LeClair to his grandpa. He didn't say anything about the coin, either. The last thing he wanted to do was explain to his grandpa that he'd taken it while snooping in his teacher's desk. As he walked along, he toyed with the coin in his pocket. *Why does Mr. LeClair keep such a valuable coin in his desk?* he thought. *And how did he get it? It's hundreds of years old, but it's shiny and in perfect condition. This must have been quite the find. My grandpa hasn't dug up anything like this in his whole life. Shouldn't it be in a museum or something?*

The sun was still high in the sky when they got to the tents, but the forest was dark and cool. Spots of sunlight trickled through the leaves, dancing on the tents.

Marvin, Lucas, and Dave started putting the camping gear into their tents. Nicole set up her own. Dave had dug out a fire pit and put rocks around it. He had also filled three buckets with water and set them nearby. The water was for making sure the fire was out before they went to bed. It was also good to have on hand in case the fire got out of control.

Once their gear was put away, Dave took them all rock hounding. He had a helmet with a headlight attached to it that helped him examine the rocks better. He also had a small brown case with tools in it. There were knives, chisels, and little brooms to dust off the dirt. Marvin's grandpa took searching for rocks very seriously. He knew about all the different types of rock in the area. He also knew about the stages of rock. Once, Dave had found a rock that was supposedly pre-diamond. Marvin had never seen him so happy.

After rock hounding, they built a fire and had some snacks. Lucas polished off a box of cookies in no time. They ate all the chips, the other box of cookies, and drank the soda within an hour.

The fire crackled in the dark woods, sending bright sparks up into the night air. Marvin looked at his glow watch—a gift from Lucas on his sixth birthday. It was nine o'clock now. It would be three more hours until midnight—the time that Marvin expected the stranger to show up. Nicole poked the fire with a long stick. She was sitting on a large tree trunk. Lucas sat on a tree trunk to her left. Marvin sat across from her. Dave was sitting to the right. They formed a square around the fire.

"Has anyone heard of the ghost of Green Hills?" Dave said. He was staring into the fire. Marvin could see the smile on his face.

"No, you haven't told us that one yet," Lucas said. The kids loved hearing Dave's stories. He knew more myths, legends, and ancient riddles than anyone else they knew. They were sure that most of them were made up.

"Yeah, Grandpa. Tell them about the ghost of Green Hills," Marvin said.

Dave poked the fire with his stick, creating a shower of sparks. He shook his head. "Nope. I shouldn't tell you. You won't be able to sleep tonight. Lucas here might even wet his pants," he said, grinning.

"Come on, Dave. We can take any story you have to dish out," Nicole said. "And Lucas hasn't wet his pants since at least…oh…Monday."

Lucas reached over and slapped her arm lightly. "Hey, that was weeks ago," he joked.

"Well, okay, if you think you can take it," Dave said. He cleared his throat and took off his tan, wide-brimmed hat. "A long time ago, when I was just a kid, I heard this story. Most people think it's true. Seems that hundreds of years ago there was a family living in these woods. Right here. Almost on the very spot we are sitting."

He stopped and looked around at the serious faces. Then he stared back into the fire. "Well, according to legend, they discovered a cave. It seemed like any other cave. The parents let their young son play in it every day while they hunted. One day, they saw a bright light coming from the cave. They quickly ran over and looked inside, just in time to see their son vanish. He simply walked into the wall and disappeared into thin air. His parents never saw him again. Some people thought there was a secret tunnel in the cave. They never found it. Rumor has it that the boy finally found his way back to the forest. Now, hundreds of years later, he wanders in the woods at night."

Everyone was silent. The woods were deadly quiet. Then Dave held a flashlight up to his chin.

"*Mwaaa ha ha ha ha ha!*" he called in a deep, bellowing voice.

Nicole screamed. Lucas fell off his log.

Marvin didn't move a muscle. Instead, he smiled and started to clap. "Ha, he got you! He's famous for his loud endings. I've seen the 'flashlight-on-the-face' trick a thousand times!"

"That's brutal, Dave. Your face looks horrible. Turn that light off," Nicole said. She rolled her eyes.

"That was awesome!" Lucas said. He got up, brushed the dirt off his shirt, and sat down again. "You totally scared the crap out of me!"

Dave turned off the flashlight and laughed. "Yeah, that used to get Marvin all the time. Only he would cry," he said.

"Hey, I was four years old," Marvin called.

They all laughed.

The group sat for a long while, watching the crackling fire. The blue, red, and orange flames flickered in the cool, dark forest.

After a while, Nicole broke the silence. "So, the story. You made that up, right?" she asked.

Dave smiled. "I don't know," he answered. "I can't remember if it's a real legend or if I made it up. I have made up so many of them through the years." He stood up. "Listen, I'm heading off to bed. If you see anything, give me a holler. Otherwise, sweet dreams."

Dave threw his stick on the fire. He told them not to add any more wood. He was going to sleep, and he didn't want the kids having a fire without an adult around. They were to pour a bucket of water on the ashes when the fire was totally out. Dave said he would get up in the night to check on it. Then he went into the big brown tent and zipped it shut.

"Goodnight," he called. "If the ghost comes by, tell him to grab a soda."

"Goodnight," they all answered.

The kids sat around the fire for a while longer. Finally, Marvin looked at his watch again. It was eleven-thirty—almost show time.

The woods were black. There was barely any light at all, except for a faint light from the moon passing through the trees. The moon was partly hidden by the dense branches. It looked like it was almost a full moon. They could also see a few stars in the dark sky.

The three of them sat quietly watching the fire until it was barely a pile of glowing embers.

The air was getting colder. Nicole had on a big sweatshirt, but the boys hadn't brought anything warm to wear and sat with their arms crossed, shivering a little.

At fifteen minutes to midnight, Marvin started to get nervous. Then he had a great idea. "Hey, you guys, it's really dark out. What if we can't see the person from over here?" he asked quietly. "If we want to find out who found the cave, why don't we go and wait for him?"

"Sit in a dark cave, waiting for a stranger? Isn't that a bit dangerous?" Nicole asked.

"No, not *in* the cave. We'll hide behind those big rocks *beside* the cave," Marvin answered. "Come on. Nobody knows that cave like we do. You're not scared, are you?"

"No, I'm not scared," said Nicole. "I just think it's dumb. But if you boys think you can handle it, let's go." She stood up and brushed her hands on her pants.

"Fine, I'll do it," Lucas said. He stood up, too. "What about Dave? If he wakes up and sees that we're gone, won't he be worried?"

"He won't wake up. Besides, we won't be very long. If he did get up and see that we weren't there, he'd call us. The cave is right over there. We would hear him," Marvin said. "Let me just peek in and make sure he's sleeping."

Marvin walked around to the front of the tent, unzipped the flap, and poked his head in. There was no one inside.

"Grandpa?" he said. No one answered.

"He's not in there?" Lucas asked.

Nicole smiled. "Bingo. I think we know who the midnight hiker is—and who has been exploring the cave."

Marvin looked around the dark forest, confused. He was shaking his head. "No. He must be rock hounding or something. Come on. Let's go."

He led the way toward the cave. He unclipped the small flashlight from his belt loop. It was difficult to walk in the dark, even though his eyes had adjusted to the darkness. Marvin pointed a small beam of light toward the ground. Lucas and Nicole followed him. Every now and then, he had to stop and shine the light straight ahead to make sure they were going the right way. They didn't have to walk very far to get to the cave. In fact, they could still see the tents through the trees. They stood at the mouth of the cave for a moment. Marvin shone his light around the inside of the cave. No one was in there. They stepped inside.

If it was dark outside, it was even darker inside the cave. It was like someone had put a hand over Marvin's eyes. He stood still for a moment and let his eyes get used to the new level of darkness. After a little while, he could at least see shapes. Now, when he looked out into the woods, it didn't seem so dark out there anymore.

"Hey, Nicole, you look great in this light," Lucas said.

"Gee, thanks. It's funny, even though I can't see you very well, I can smell you just fine," Nicole shot back.

"Okay, nobody is in here. Let's go back outside and hide out behind the big rocks beside the cave. No one will be able to see us there," Marvin said.

"Marvin, no one is even coming in here. Unless, of course, it's Grandpa Dave," Nicole said.

"We'll see. Come on. And keep a lookout for a light in the forest," Marvin said. If it *was* his grandpa, he would be relieved. After all, he didn't mind if his grandpa was investigating the cave. *Why would he keep it a secret, though?* he wondered.

Lucas and Nicole followed Marvin and his flashlight out of the cave to their hiding place. All three of them crouched down so that they were totally hidden behind the rocks. Marvin peeked around one side, looking into the cave. Lucas peeked around the other side. Nicole could see through the crack between the rocks.

They stared into the darkness for what seemed like a long time. Marvin could hear the sounds of owls hooting, crickets chirping, and small animals scampering over the forest floor. He thought it sounded spooky, but he also liked it.

"My legs hurt," Lucas whispered. His knees were bent as he hid. He looked like a back catcher crouched behind home plate.

"Then sit on the ground," Marvin said. He was kneeling, and the stones on the ground were digging into his shins.

"Can we go now? Obviously no one is coming. Your midnight hiker is not the person who found our cave. We are the only ones stupid enough to come to a cave at midnight," Nicole said.

Marvin pushed the glow button on his watch again so the face would light up. It was almost midnight. "Just wait a few more minutes," he whispered.

When he looked into the forest, he gasped. Far in the distance was a tiny dot of light.

"Look at that," Marvin whispered. "There's a light way over there."

"It's probably just Dave looking for us with his flashlight," Lucas said.

"No, he would be calling us by now," Marvin said. He squinted his eyes but couldn't tell who the person was.

The little light got closer and closer. Before long, the light was pointing straight into the cave.

The kids ducked as the person walked past the rocks and into the cave. The flashlight illuminated the dark opening. Marvin smiled. Now there was no doubt about the hiker's identity.

The three friends stayed hidden and were completely silent. Nicole's eyes were wide with shock. Lucas' mouth was hanging open. Mr. LeClair had gone into the cave.

A minute later he came running out again.

Lucas, Marvin, and Nicole didn't move a muscle. They didn't even seem to breathe. Marvin waited quite a long time before he dared to stand up. He crept quietly toward the cave entrance and looked into the darkness. Then he turned around to look behind him. He could see a flashlight beam far away. It was getting smaller and smaller. Marvin sighed. Mr. LeClair was gone.

"Come on out. He's gone," Marvin whispered toward the rocks. "He didn't see us."

Lucas and Nicole came out slowly and walked toward the cave.

"What...was...that?" Nicole asked.

"I knew it. It was Mr. LeClair, and he's after something in that cave. I bet it's the carving," Marvin said.

"But why would he come all the way here just to run in and out of the cave for a minute?" Lucas asked. "It doesn't make sense."

Marvin ran into the darkness of the cave. He lit his tiny flashlight and looked around for a minute. He wanted to see if Mr. LeClair left any clues behind. When he came out of the cave, he was holding something.

"Guess what I found on the ground in the cave?" Marvin asked.

"I'm too tired to guess," Nicole said. "Spill it."

Marvin held out his hand. It was a coin.

"That's the coin you got from Mr. LeClair's desk," Lucas said.

"Think again," Marvin said. He opened his other hand to reveal an identical coin. "This must be the second coin from his collection."

"Why would he take his coin into the cave? Didn't you say he only had three of them? He is going to lose it when he finds out this one is gone, too," Nicole said.

"Maybe these coins have something to do with the cave," Marvin said. "And now he only has one left."

Lucas, Marvin, and Nicole crept away quietly. Marvin was afraid that Mr. LeClair might come back. He was afraid of what the teacher would do to them if he caught them spying on him.

Marvin had never been afraid of the forest before, even when it was dark. Now, every sound in the dark woods gave him the creeps. He walked slowly and quietly, straining his eyes to try and see Mr. LeClair's flashlight in the distance.

When the three of them got back to their tents, they went inside and zipped them shut. Dave came strolling back shortly after, whistling quietly. Marvin peeked out of his tent and saw that Dave had a bag of rocks in his hand. *That's where he was*, Marvin thought. *I should have known.* He closed his tent and snuggled into his sleeping bag. In no time, he was fast asleep.

In the morning, after a breakfast of Dave's famous fried eggs on the campfire, it was time to pack up. Dave had no idea the kids had gone into the cave the night before. No one said a word to him about Mr. LeClair. Marvin felt bad keeping a secret from his grandpa. They were friends. He knew that of all adults, his grandpa wouldn't laugh at them. Still, Marvin thought maybe something like this would make his grandpa think twice about taking him into the forest. He was afraid that Dave would tell his parents. Then it would all be over. He would never be allowed into the forest again.

They all helped Dave carry his camping gear to his car, which was parked at the end of Marvin's street. Then they went back for their own stuff.

When Dave drove away, they walked to Marvin's house. Lucas and Nicole called their parents to let them know that they were okay. They decided to hang out at Marvin's house for the day. He had a basement full of video games and CDs. They hung out there all the time. Once they were downstairs, they could talk in privacy.

"Pretty wild last night, huh?" Lucas said. "I couldn't sleep all night."

"Me neither," Marvin said. "What do you suppose he was doing in there?"

"Who cares?" Nicole said. "It's just a cave." She sounded grumpy.

"Who's a widdle gwumpy because she was wrong?" Lucas teased in a baby voice. "Are you just a teeny bit sad that Mr. LeClair is, in fact, a total weirdo?"

"He hikes at night and is interested in an ancient cave. So what? So are we. It doesn't prove a thing, okay?" Nicole answered.

"It proves that something is up with that cave. It proves that something is going on with those coins. He must know something we don't. He keeps going there at midnight, and the carving says something about midnight. Don't you want to know what he's up to?" Marvin asked.

Nicole shrugged her shoulders. "A little…I guess…but I really like him. He's a good teacher! Maybe he's just trying to figure out what that carving in the wall really means. Is that so bad?"

"Whatever. I want to know what he knows about our cave," Marvin answered. He got up and put a CD in the stereo. Then he sat back down.

"Me too. Are you thinking what I'm thinking?" Lucas asked with a wicked grin.

"I'm afraid so," said Marvin. He had the same stupid grin on his face.

Nicole rolled her eyes. "Oh no. Not another one of your plans."

"Oh yes. Methinks we have a mystery to solve," Lucas said. "What say you, Sir Marvin?"

"I say, we're going in!" Marvin answered. "Tonight. Who's in?"

Lucas agreed right away.

Nicole took some convincing. "Well, I can't very well leave the brains of this operation to you two," she said finally. "Besides, I want to see with my own eyes what Mr. LeClair is doing in the cave. I'm in."

That night, Marvin said goodnight to his parents. He went to his room, like he always did. His parents played cards, like they always did on Saturday nights. By eleven o'clock they were in bed. Right on schedule.

Marvin, Lucas, and Nicole had agreed to meet at the end of Marvin's street at fifteen minutes to midnight. They had to do it without getting caught. Marvin left a note on his pillow. It read: "Okay, you caught me. I'm out in the forest, checking out the cave. I know I'm probably grounded for life."

That was just in case his parents woke up and came into his room. He figured he should at least let them know where he was, even if he was going to get grounded. They never came into his room at night, but stranger things had happened. If his parents did come in and he was gone, that would be it. He would be in the biggest trouble of his life. But he had to do it sometime. He had to figure out what Mr. LeClair was doing in the cave. And it had to be done at midnight.

At eleven-thirty, Marvin quietly got out of bed and put his ear to the door. He heard nothing but his father snoring. He tiptoed to his window and slowly slid it open without making a noise. He climbed up onto his desk. In a moment he was on the roof, just above the garage. He slid across the roof above the porch, where the front lawn rose up into a hill. Then he jumped down and landed with a thud on the lawn, dropping and rolling on the grass.

Marvin had done that trick a few times when he was younger. It always got him into big trouble. Not as much trouble as it would this time. This time, it was the dead of night.

He lay there for a moment to make sure no one saw him. Then he got up, walked to the end of the front yard, and turned right. Within seconds he was at the end of the street.

He waited a few minutes at the entrance to the forest. His watch read 11:45. *Lucas and Nicole had better hurry up,* Marvin thought impatiently. He didn't want to miss his chance. He wanted to get to the cave by midnight, and he planned to go with, or without, Lucas and Nicole. Of course, he really preferred to go "with."

Marvin heard the sound of footsteps, and he breathed a sigh of relief. Then he thought of Mr. LeClair, and for a moment, he was scared. *What if it's Mr. LeClair on his way to the cave?* Marvin didn't want to get caught in the woods all by himself. He was relieved to find that the footsteps he heard belonged to friends, not foes. Lucas and Nicole were right behind him.

"Hey, I was wondering if you guys were going to make it," Marvin whispered. "We'd better hurry. I don't want our 'friend' to see us out here."

"Yeah, that's what I was thinking," Nicole said. "The point of this mission is to spy on Mr. LeClair, not to let him catch us in the dark woods."

"I know. Let's get going. We can hide out in the cave until midnight. If Mr. LeClair comes, keep down. I want to see what he is doing in there this time," Marvin said.

They walked through the forest, guided again by Marvin's flashlight. When they reached the cave, it was 11:57. Exactly three minutes until midnight. They got into the cave just in time. Marvin peeked back out the entrance and saw a tiny light in the forest again.

"We've got company," he whispered. They quickly hid behind the huge rocks at the back of the cave. Marvin checked his watch. 11:58.

The sound of footsteps got closer and closer, and soon a light flickered through the cave. Marvin, Lucas, and Nicole stayed hidden behind the rocks, frozen in fear. They watched from the shadows as Mr. LeClair fumbled with something in his pocket. Marvin couldn't quite see what he had in his hand. Then Mr. LeClair walked toward the old carving in the stone wall and held his hand up to the wall.

Slowly, a dim dot of light appeared on the cave wall. The dot of light got bigger and bigger. Soon, it was whirling in circles. The wall got bright as the whirling circles got larger. The air in the cave seemed to hum, like bees in a hive.

Marvin's mouth dropped open. He couldn't believe what he was seeing. Within seconds a huge, spinning circle of light had formed on the wall.

Suddenly, Mr. LeClair was sucked into the stone wall! In an instant, he was gone. The glowing light quickly died down. The spinning circles stopped. Now there was no one in the cave but Marvin, Lucas, and Nicole.

"Oh *crap!*" Lucas whispered loudly. "*Run!*"

They jumped up and took off out of the cave as quickly as they could, tripping over rocks as they darted out into the darkness. The thin beam of Marvin's flashlight led the way. Lucas stumbled and fell on the ground, hitting the ground with a thud. Nicole stopped to make sure he was okay, and then they kept running. Marvin had never run so fast in his life. He headed right into the heart of the dark forest. When they were far enough away, they stopped.

Marvin was panting. "Did you see that?"

"Um, I think we all saw it. In fact, I think I almost peed my pants," Lucas answered, his voice shaking. "What just happened in there? Mr. LeClair totally vanished."

"Where did he go?" Marvin wondered. "How could he just disappear like that?"

"You know, I hate to admit this, but it sounds kind of like the legend Dave told us in the forest that night," Nicole said, trying to catch her breath. "The one about the kid who disappeared in the cave and never came back."

"Yeah, except this time he seemed to want to go. That circle of light must be some kind of…opening," Marvin said.

"What do you mean?" Nicole asked.

"I mean, somehow Mr. LeClair went into the circle, and he went *through* the wall," Marvin answered.

"To where?" Lucas asked.

"I don't know. Maybe another world. Maybe another *time*," Marvin answered. He looked from one shocked face to the other. He couldn't quite believe it himself, but he could think of no other explanation.

"Time travel. You think this has to do with time travel?" Nicole said. She was sounding panicky. Her voice was quivering.

"Well, how else do you explain it? Obviously Mr. LeClair went somewhere. We all know that the wall is made of solid rock. And you can't deny seeing him walk right into that fuzzy light and disappear," Marvin said.

He was starting to get excited. He had read lots of books about time travel. He knew that there were plenty of things in this world that could not be explained. He figured there was life on other planets. Why not time travel? Maybe the cave was some kind of doorway...maybe it was a portal to another world.

"Did you see him hold up his hand to that carving? It never does anything when you hold your hand up to it," Nicole said. An owl hooted behind her and she jumped a little.

"He took something out of his pocket. He must have had it in his hand when he touched the wall," Marvin said.

"But what was it? And how would he know where or when he was going? He never said 'Um, I'd like to go back to 1814 please.' Unless he had a piece of paper with a date on it in his hand," Nicole said. She laughed.

Lucas laughed, too. "Yeah, like a ticket. One ticket to time travel. Oh sorry, sir, you have the wrong date on that. We are going to have to send you back to 1743 instead. Have a nice trip!"

Marvin was deep in thought. He stood with his hands in his pockets and closed his eyes. *What could Mr. LeClair be using to open the portal? It must be something small. Something that would fit in his pocket, like a token.*

He felt around in his own pocket. All he had in his pocket were Mr. LeClair's coins. He pulled them out and looked closely at them. They looked shiny, but they were obviously from a long time ago. They had been made during the reign of King Charles VII, which meant they were around 600 years old. Marvin couldn't figure out how a coin so old could look so new.

He closed his eyes and imagined the cave. He could see the carving on the wall in his mind. Suddenly, he gasped. "Wait! I think I know how Mr. LeClair did it!"

"How?" Lucas asked.

"What if he used a coin to activate the portal? Maybe that's what Mr. LeClair took out of his pocket. Maybe he went back to the year the coin was made," Marvin said. His face was tingling, and his heart was racing. Suddenly, it seemed to make perfect sense.

Lucas and Nicole looked at each other and then back at Marvin.

"Are you serious?" Lucas asked. "Let me see those coins." He took them from Marvin and looked at them carefully. "They don't have dates on them. How would he know what year he was going to?" He handed the coins back to Marvin.

"They changed the coin designs slightly every few years. Someone who knows about this stuff would be able to find out the date of the coin. Besides, the coins were struck at many different mints. You know, the factories where coins were made. Not all mints operated in every year," Marvin answered.

"Dude, you have to get a life or something. You have way too much historical knowledge," Lucas said. He shook his head.

"We learned all this in class, bonehead," Marvin said. "If you actually paid attention, you'd learn something. Remember Jason's project on medieval money? And anyway, Mr. LeClair would know what year his coins are from. He's crazy about medieval stuff."

Lucas shrugged his shoulders. "I guess it could have been a coin. That would make sense...if any of this makes any sense at all," he said.

"I can't believe it. This is so awesome! Time travel. Can you imagine that?" Marvin said in an excited voice.

"Shhh. If anyone hears us, we're all in trouble," Nicole whispered. She looked back into the darkness. "So, you really think he used the medieval coins to vanish into the wall?" she asked.

They all laughed a bit. It sounded so strange.

"Fine. We have no proof that he used the coins to get through the wall. But he did take something small out of his pocket. And he did hold it up to the carving. Come on! This is huge!" Marvin said

"So, if he only had one coin left, and he just used it tonight, is he..." Nicole's voice trailed off, her question unspoken.

Marvin nodded his head. "He's gone forever," he said.

There was silence in the forest. It didn't last very long.

"Yes!" Lucas shouted. "We are finally rid of that guy. I never thought I'd say this before, but I hope we get a nice, normal teacher next year."

Marvin smiled. "Yeah, this is great! I would have died if I got him for homeroom next year. Now we never have to see his face again, thanks to these coins. Huh. Who knew?"

"Shhh!" Nicole whispered with a scowl. She looked around. "Listen, those coins are cursed or something. I don't want any of us disappearing into a wall. We have to get rid of them. Now that Mr. LeClair is gone, we don't have to put them back in his desk. I think we should bury them. Deep."

Marvin opened his hand. Two coins lay on his palm. He could barely see them sparkle in the moonlight. "Really? But they're so..."

"They're so bad luck, Marvin," Nicole interrupted.

"For once I have to agree with Nic," Lucas said. "Whatever happened in that cave, it wasn't good. Those coins caused a person to vanish. We can't risk having them around. They're too powerful. Who knows what else they can do? We should bury them. Right here in the woods."

Marvin sighed. He had finally found something truly special. Something truly ancient.

GD G.D. Fast

For a minute he wondered if King Charles VII himself had touched the coins. He didn't want to let them go. Still, he didn't want anyone getting hurt, either. It seemed like he had no choice but to bury them forever.

74

Marvin bent down to the ground. He started digging a hole with a stick. Lucas and Nicole looked at each other and smiled a little. Marvin knew that they didn't want this adventure to end, either. But they had no choice. They found out the secret of the coins. And a deadly secret it was. The problem was, they now had more questions than ever before.

They had figured out the secret of the medieval coins, but now they had a million questions about Mr. LeClair. Who was he, and why had he disappeared into the cave wall? Was he a brave discoverer of scientific wonders or a horrible freak from another world? Now he was gone. For Lucas, Marvin, and Nicole, it was time to put the mystery to bed.

The dirt was damp and cold. Marvin dug down as far as he could. Then he dropped the two small objects into the deep grave. He pushed the pile of loose earth into the hole, filling it completely. Then he stood up and sighed.

Lucas patted Marvin lightly on his back. "I know how you feel, buddy. But this is the only thing we can do."

Marvin nodded, but he didn't say a word.

Then, Lucas stepped forward and stomped down the dirt on the hole. The pile of dirt flattened out. There was barely a trace of a burial site. When he was done, they stood for a moment. Marvin dropped his stick and stepped on it.

"Well, I guess this is finally over," Nicole said quietly. "We should get back home."

"Yeah, come on," Lucas said. Marvin lit his flashlight. They followed the thin beam through the forest and back to Marvin's street.

"Don't worry, Marvin," Nicole said gently. "You'll find something else that's special some day."

"I know," Marvin said.

Marvin waved good-bye as he got to his house. He walked up to the front porch and climbed up the trellis. Then he quietly walked across the roof of the porch until he was at his bedroom window. His window was still open. No lights were on in the house except for the little lamp in his bedroom. His parents never even knew he was gone.

Marvin climbed through the window and onto his desk. Then he stepped down to the floor and closed the window.

For a few minutes, Marvin stared out into the starry darkness. He pictured the cave. He thought about Mr. LeClair holding the coin to the carving. He could picture the swirling lights on the wall and Mr. LeClair disappearing. Then Marvin sighed. He sat down on his bed for a moment.

I can't believe they wanted to bury the coins forever, he thought. Then he smiled and pulled something out of his pocket. He looked at his hand in the lamplight. The two coins lay side by side.

These are way too special to leave buried in the ground. They can become part of my collection, he thought. *Besides…you never know…*

Marvin opened his bottom desk drawer. He placed the coins inside a small wooden box. Then he closed the drawer and took one last look out his window into the dark night. Finally, he turned out his lamp and climbed into bed.

On Monday morning, the June sky was bright and sunny. Marvin got dressed for school and went down the road. His short, blond hair was combed neatly. He slung his backpack over his shoulder. He was ready for a great day. A great last week of grade five. After all, Mr. LeClair was finally gone.

"Hey, Marvin!" Lucas called. He waited for Lucas to catch up with him at the pathway that led to the soccer field.

"Hey!" Marvin answered. "What's up?"

"Not much, my friend," Lucas said. He put his baseball cap on backward. His red-blond hair poked out of the hole. "I guess we have some free time today, huh?" he asked, smiling.

"Oh yeah! I forgot about that! If Mr. LeClair is gone, there won't be any social studies class. All right!" he said. They high-fived each other. Marvin always had to reach up a bit to high five with Lucas.

The boys walked across the soccer field and onto the pavement by the school. They looked around for Nicole. There was always a chance that she would show up on time for school. Then again, she was usually late. Looking across the field, Marvin could see a girl with long, brown hair from a distance. He squinted. The closer she got, the more he was sure it was Nicole.

"Good morning," she said quietly when she reached the boys. She let out a yawn.

"Well, well, well," Lucas said. "Aren't you bright and chipper today. What happened? All out of Chocoflakes this morning?"

Nicole smiled a bit. "No. I just didn't sleep well this weekend."

"I know what you mean," Marvin said. "Ever since we saw Mr. LeClair disappear into the cave wall Saturday night, I haven't been able to sleep.

I keep thinking about the coins, and the cave, and…you know." He looked around to make sure no one was listening.

"No kidding. I still can't believe that the wall opened up like that and pulled him in. I still can't believe he's gone for good," Nicole said.

"Well, I can believe it. We saw it with our own eyes," Lucas added. "Another high five?"

Marvin smiled. He slapped Lucas' hand. Then he slapped Nicole's hand. "Yup, that wacko teacher is gone for good. I can't tell you how happy I am that he's not coming back. I'm so sick of his stupid medieval history lessons. And I swear, he *did* have a sharp knife on his desk last week. I can picture it. Silver handle, green jewel. He might have used it, too. He was so weird."

"At least those medieval coins are gone. I'm glad we buried them in the forest. They were major bad luck," Nicole said quietly. She fixed the sparkly barrette that was stuck in her hair. "Look what happened to Mr. LeClair!"

"Yeah, if it was, in fact, those coins that caused him to disappear in the cave. I'm glad we're rid of them now," Lucas said. He put on his sunglasses and waved to some girls across the playground.

Marvin didn't say anything. He thought about the two medieval coins hidden in his desk drawer. Lucas and Nicole had no idea that he had kept the coins instead of burying them in the forest. Now, they were part of Marvin's new collection.

Not his rock collection, but his new collection of historical artifacts.

His grandpa would love it. Too bad he couldn't tell his grandpa what the coins could do. He couldn't risk his grandpa telling his parents. They wouldn't be impressed that Marvin was sneaking around a forest at night, not to mention the disappearing teacher thing. Marvin would probably get in huge trouble. And if Lucas and Nicole found out, they'd be mad that he hadn't actually buried the coins.

The bell rang, and Marvin headed toward the school. Lucas and Nicole were right behind him. Kids loudly pushed their way through the doors, and the teachers tried to quiet them down, as usual. This was the last week of school before the summer holidays, and life was good.

Lucas, Marvin, and Nicole got to the end of the hall. Before they even got a chance to go to their homerooms, the three friends stopped dead. Other students knocked and bumped them, but they didn't move. They were all looking down the hall toward the library, holding their breath.

"He's back!" Lucas hit Marvin in the arm, but Marvin was already staring at the man down the hall. It was Mr. LeClair.

"Ow! I know! I can see that. I'm standing right here!" Marvin said, turning to give Lucas a dirty look. He couldn't believe it. *How in the world could this have happened?* he wondered.

Nicole was frozen to the spot.

Lucas waved a hand in front of her face. "Hey. Sunshine. You there?"

"What is he doing here? He…" Nicole said.

"He came back," Marvin said quietly.

⊰10⊱

"**Midnight** *fly, by twenty-four, back in time no time shall pass. Miss the door in twenty-four and no more,*" Marvin whispered. It was the cryptic message carved into the cave wall. He knew it off by heart. "Okay, let's see. You have to fly by midnight, in twenty-four hours. No time will pass. Miss the door and no more. What door? And what's 'no more'?"

Marvin, Lucas, and Nicole were sitting in Marvin's basement. The day had been a blur. They had avoided Mr. LeClair all day. Now, they were trying to figure out how all of this had happened. Why was Mr. LeClair back?

"Maybe *you* are no more," Lucas said.

"So if you miss the door in twenty-four hours, you will disappear?" Nicole asked.

"No, if you miss the door in twenty-four hours, you are *no more*. You'll die," Lucas said.

"Well, if you fly at midnight and have to be back in twenty-four hours or you won't exist, you must be able to get back," Marvin said. "That stupid portal must work both ways. You must be able to come back. Crap! I never thought of that! If he used a coin to disappear from here, he must have used another coin from the present and traveled back again!"

"Okay, so if he travels back within twenty-four hours, no time passes? He comes back a few seconds later?" Lucas asked.

"Maybe the portal only works at midnight. *Midnight fly, by twenty-four, back in time no time shall pass.* You return within twenty-four hours and no time passes. You return on the same day you leave, just around midnight," Marvin answered.

"You mean he leaves through the wall on April 14 at midnight. He goes back in time to, say April 14, 1801 at midnight. He hangs out there for days, and then he comes back to April 14, right after midnight?" Nicole asked.

"No. *Miss the door in twenty-four and no more.* You must have to come back on the same day, or you can't come back at all," said Marvin. "I guess the only way to return at all is to make it back to the portal within twenty-four hours. Then *no time shall pass*. Maybe you have a twenty-four-hour window."

"How is that possible?" Nicole asked.

"Um, Nic? We *are* talking about time travel here. At this point, anything is possible," Lucas said, shaking his head. "If no time passed, no one would even know you were gone. You would have two lives."

"I'm totally freaked out," Nicole said. "You think he does this every night? He travels back and forth in time? What about the coins? He doesn't have any left."

"Maybe he grabbed a few more from his piggy bank, Nic. Maybe he brought some more back with him," Lucas said. "The question now is what do we do?"

"We do nothing. We leave it alone. He time travels. Well...it could be worse. So what?" Nicole stood up and walked around. She took a few deep breaths. Then she got a drink from the fridge in the basement. Her hand waved frantically as she fanned herself.

"So what?" Marvin repeated. "Nicole, we have a wacko teacher who disappears into cave walls. We're pretty sure that he uses his medieval coins to activate the portal. Then he comes back. Don't you think this is a bit of a problem? This guy is way out there. Now we *really* have to get rid of him!"

"What are we supposed to do? Go back to his classroom and steal some more coins? Then go to the cave and try it ourselves? Huh?" Nicole asked in a squeaky voice.

"I didn't steal it. I accidentally took it. Anyway, we don't have to find another coin," Marvin said seriously.

"There's no way we can dig up those coins again. We'll never find them. It was the middle of the night," Lucas said. He narrowed his eyes and looked at Marvin. "Or do you know where those coins are?"

Marvin stood up and went upstairs. When he came back, he held out the two medieval coins.

Nicole gasped.

Lucas grinned. "Looks like we're back in business," he said.

That night, Marvin waited for Lucas and Nicole at the entrance to the forest. This time, they were going to follow Mr. LeClair wherever he went. Marvin just wasn't sure if Nicole was going to show up. She was pretty angry that Marvin had lied about burying the coins. He insisted he hadn't lied. He just never said anything. Anyway, now they needed those coins. And Marvin was pretty sure that Nicole wouldn't miss out on an adventure. She hated being left out.

Lucas and Nicole showed up right on time. It was dark and quiet in the forest. When they reached the cave, they ran inside and hid behind the rock just like they had planned.

Mr. LeClair showed up right on time, too. They watched him reach into his pocket and then hold his hand up to the wall. Nothing happened.

Marvin couldn't check the time. He did not want Mr. LeClair to see the tiny glow from his watch. Instead, he held his breath and waited.

Soon, the tiny yellow dot of light appeared on the cave wall. It swirled bigger and bigger, until it was a huge swirling circle the size of an adult. Mr. LeClair walked into it and was gone. Then the light died down.

Marvin jumped up and ran over to the carving. "Come on, you guys. We only have a minute. We have to go now, while we can. Lucas, put your arms around my waist. Nicole, you hold onto Lucas. We'll all go in together," he said.

"Wait a minute," Nicole said in a panic-stricken voice. "Does anyone have a coin with this year on it?"

"Oh, crap," said Marvin. "I didn't think of that. We won't be able to get back without it."

They all fumbled quickly through their pockets. Marvin's flashlight lit up his hand. He had coins from last year, and a few years ago, but none from this year. Lucas held open his hand. Marvin shone the light on it.

"Aha, here's one." Lucas put it back safely in his pocket. "Go, Marvin. Hold up your coin."

Lucas put his arms around Marvin's waist, and Nicole put hers around Lucas. Marvin grasped the medieval coin in his right hand. He pressed the coin against the carving. His hands were sweaty. He hoped he wouldn't drop the coin on the ground. His heart was racing.

Marvin felt a tingling in his hand. Suddenly, a dot of light appeared on the cave wall. It grew larger, and it was soon a huge swirling circle of light. He closed his eyes and took a giant step toward the wall, pulling his friends along with him.

❧ 11 ❧

Marvin felt like he had been puked onto the floor by some giant animal. Lucas and Nicole landed on top of him. Marvin gasped for air. Lucas was a heavy guy.

"Get…off…me," Marvin panted. His cheek was pressed into the dirt. Lucas and Nicole rolled over and got up. Marvin shook his head and stood up, too. They dusted off their clothes and looked around, squinting.

"Okay. This is weird," Lucas said.

Marvin looked around the dim, narrow space. Torches were attached to the walls. They lit up the darkness. It looked like the inside of the cave, only it was bigger. It was a hallway. Marvin could see someone disappear around the corner. He figured it was Mr. LeClair. Marvin stood quietly for a moment.

Thankfully, Mr. LeClair did not seem to notice that anyone else came through the wall behind him.

Marvin crept down the hallway, looking around. The floor was made of dirt and stone. The walls were made of stones. There were wooden beams across the ceiling. He stopped when he came to the end of the hallway. He could hear noises coming from another hall, far to the left. They were moans. The moaning was echoing down the dark, cold hall.

Marvin slowly peeked his head around the corner. He could see metal bars and a boy sitting in a wooden chair just past the bars. It seemed as though this was a dungeon of some kind.

Marvin smiled. He was thrilled that they had made it back in time. He was also terrified. And excited. And scared. He didn't know what to think.

He and his friends had in fact landed in medieval times. It was exactly what he had hoped for. The problem was, now what were they supposed to do? And where exactly were they?

Marvin went back down the dark hall to the spot where they had landed on the floor. Lucas and Nicole were still standing there.

"Where are we?" Nicole whispered. She tidied her long brown hair.

"I'm not sure, but I think we are in a dungeon," Marvin answered.

"What do you mean?" Nicole asked. "Where? What kind of dungeon?"

"I don't know, but there are a few jail cells down that hallway," Marvin said. He was pointing to his left. "There's also a guard outside of one of the cells. I think this is the basement of a castle."

"So we actually went back in time?" Lucas asked loudly.

"Shhhhhhh," Nicole whispered. "Do you want the guard to hear you?"

"Sorry," Lucas said quietly.

"I'm not exactly sure what year we are in. But I can tell you this—we aren't in Green Park anymore. And this sure isn't any basement I've ever seen," Marvin whispered.

"Well, what do we do now?" Lucas asked.

"Let's try to sneak past the guard and look around a bit," Marvin said. "I'm dying to know what the rest of this place looks like."

"Don't say the word 'dying,' please," Nicole whispered. She brushed her hair out of her face. "And what if that guard sees us?"

"Do you have a better idea?" Marvin asked.

"Yes, let's get out of here," Nicole answered. She turned around to face the stone wall behind them. There was a design in the stone similar to the one in the cave they had just left.

"No way. We can't just leave. Let's just look around for a while, Nic. Besides, the portal only works at midnight," Marvin said.

Lucas took out his coin and held it in his hand. He pressed his hand and the coin against the carving on the wall. Nothing happened. "He's right. We probably have a full day to spend here before we can go back," he said.

"My mom is going to have a fit," Nicole whined. She looked like she was about to cry.

"Nicole, *back in time no time shall pass*, remember? We'll go back at midnight tomorrow, and it will be like we were only gone a minute. The only trouble you'll get in will be for sneaking out into the woods at night. You won't be missing for days or anything," Marvin said.

"Oh yeah. Okay," Nicole sighed. "Well, if we have twenty-four hours to kill, we had better get out of here. I don't want to spend the whole day in a dungeon."

Lucas and Nicole followed Marvin to the other end of the hallway. Firelight flickered from the torches on the walls. The firelight was the same color as Lucas' hair, making the blond tips on his short, red hair look like flames.

At the end of the hallway was another hall. To the left, there were jail cells. To the right, it was just dark and quiet. Marvin pointed to the hallway that went right. He didn't want to go past the guard or the prisoners in the cells. He had no idea, though, what waited at the end of the dark hallway on the right.

Slowly they tiptoed around the corner and began edging their way down the other hall. Marvin kept looking over his shoulder. The guard didn't move. He seemed to be sleeping. Nicole followed him, and then Lucas. When they got halfway down the dark hallway, they could see a set of stairs up ahead. They were almost there. At least the guard hadn't caught them in their first five minutes in the castle.

They barely made a sound as they walked to the stairway. Just as Marvin was about to take a step up, he heard a noise right behind them. He gasped and turned around.

"En garde!" a voice said loudly.

Marvin stood frozen. He could see Nicole and Lucas out of the corner of his eye. Lucas had his eyes closed tightly, and his face was scrunched up in panic. Nicole was staring at the strange boy in front of them. She didn't say a word.

The boy with the long, shiny sword smiled and bowed. He said something to them in French. Nicole answered him in French. They both smiled.

"Welcome to France," the boy said in English. He spoke with a thick French accent. "My name is Louis. I am at your service."

Lucas opened one eye, then the other. He breathed a sigh of relief. Nicole sighed, too.

"Why aren't you afraid of us?" Marvin asked.

"Because you have no weapons," Louis answered with certainty. "Where do you come from? Your clothes are strange." He looked suspiciously at Lucas. "Are you a witch? Certainly those with red hair are thought to be witches."

"Thanks a lot, buddy. No. We, uh, come from the future," Lucas said.

The boy stared at them, frowning. He raised his long sword.

Marvin kicked Lucas with his foot. "What he means is, we've come from Britain, where...we have no future," Marvin said. He couldn't tell the boy where they really came from. North America wasn't officially discovered in the 1400s. The only country he could think of was Britain.

Lucas and Nicole started to laugh. They sounded nervous. Marvin was afraid that the boy would think they were spies. They were, after all, sneaking around the basement of a castle. Marvin was worried that Louis would lock them all up in the dungeons right behind them. Then they wouldn't be able to find Mr. LeClair, and they'd never make it back home at midnight.

Instead the boy smiled. "Brilliant. So you have traveled all the way from Britain? My father is a noble. He has told me all about different countries. He has taught me much. I know how to read, you know." He looked very proud of himself. Marvin wondered what he was so proud of. He definitely looked old enough to read.

"Listen, we, um, kind of ran away from...a really bad knight...and we have to hide out for a while," Marvin said. He watched Louis eye them up and down, a funny look on his face. "Our clothes are different from yours, I know. We really don't want to get caught by the bad knight. Do you think you could lend us some clothing?"

The boy nodded. "I understand. How terrible that you are being chased. You must tell me all about your travels. But first, we must find you something else to wear," Louis said. "People from Britain wear strange clothes, *oui?* It is a good idea to change so no one else finds out about you."

"Why? What would they do to us?" Lucas asked. Marvin almost didn't want to know.

"Burn you at the stake, of course," Louis answered calmly. "They would believe that you are coming from another land as a spy. Haven't you heard of Joan of Arc?"

"Yes! She was burnt at the stake in 1431, right? After she helped France win the war, England captured her. The English burned her at the stake as a spy," Marvin answered.

"*Oui.* They also thought she was a witch because she said that God spoke to her. Now wait here *un moment.* I have some clothes that belong to the prisoners. Some of the owners died a long time ago. They wouldn't mind you wearing them," Louis said. He went down the hall again to the jail cells. Then he came back quickly with an armload of clothes.

"Here, wear this," the boy said. "Why don't you go down there and change your clothes? There is a pile of straw near the chair there. Bury your old clothes beneath it. No one but me and a few other guards come down here. Your things will be safe," Louis said. He pointed down the hall to where the cells were located.

Lucas and Nicole walked slowly down the hall. Nicole turned down the dark hallway where they first "landed." Lucas kept going straight. They both quickly got dressed in the dark.

Marvin went down the dark hallway and turned a corner. He pulled off his shirt and put it on the pile of straw beside him. He tugged on the long, scratchy red shirt Louis had given him. The pants were even worse. Marvin felt like he was wearing thick tights. He slipped on long, leather boots that went up over his knees and up to his thighs.

When he was dressed, he shoved his own clothes under the straw and walked back to Louis. Marvin felt better when he saw what Lucas was wearing—thick brown tights and a long shirt with puffy sleeves and a rope tied around his waist. Nicole was wearing a long blue dress. It had ruffles around the wrists and a sash around the waist. Marvin didn't want to know why that dress was in the dungeons. None of them dared to laugh.

"Why are you helping us?" Marvin asked Louis. "Shouldn't you be defending the place and locking us up?"

"Oh good, Marvin. Give him some ideas," Nicole said.

The boy smiled at Nicole. "To be truthful, I would like some company. My duty is to help Sir

Jean the Fierce. I am to learn from him. But he is away for a few days. I was not to go with him. I was left behind to take odd jobs at the castle until Sir Jean returned. Besides, you are all of my years or younger, *n'est-ce pas?* And you have no weapons. What threat could you be?"

"Well, we, um, kind of got lost, coming all the way from Britain and all, and ended up down here. Can you tell us where we are?" Nicole asked.

"You are in the castle of King Charles VII. Surely you knew this when you entered. This is the biggest castle in the land!" the boy answered. He placed his sword into his leather belt, which was tied around his waist. His long shirt was the color of wood. He wore tight stockings as pants, just like the ones he had given Marvin and Lucas. His messy brown hair grew just past his ears. It was long enough to brush the back of his shirt collar.

"What do you do around here?" Marvin asked.

"I am a squire for Sir Jean the Fierce. He is a knight in the King's court."

"Hey, that's funny. My name is Marvin McKnight," Marvin said.

Louis' eyes bugged out and his mouth fell open. Marvin looked to his left and his right. No one was there. He wondered what this boy was staring at.

"So you are a knight? *C'est fantastique!* And so young! I have to work years more to earn that title. I must get you a sword at once!" Louis said.

Marvin started to laugh a little. "No no, I'm not a knight, that's just my last name."

Louis stared at him.

"You know. This is Lucas Maxwell and Nicole Baker. I'm Marvin McKnight," Marvin said.

Louis looked very confused. "So you are not a knight, but they call you Marvin McKnight?" he asked. "And Lucas Maxwell. He is not the son of Maxwell?"

"*Riiiiiiiiight*," Marvin answered.

"Then Nicole Baker would not be a baker at all?" he asked.

Marvin laughed. "No."

"Hmm. That is very unusual. Around here, your surname refers to the work you do, or to your father's name, or to your character," Louis said. "Like Sir Jean the Fierce."

"So who are you? Louis Squire?" Marvin asked. He was joking.

"*Oui*," Louis answered seriously.

"Oh," Marvin said. He stopped laughing.

A loud moan came from the direction of the prison cells. Nicole looked over her shoulder with a worried look.

Louis looked at her strangely. "You do not need to worry. They cannot get free," he said.

"No, it's just that I feel sorry for them," Nicole said. "What did they do to be locked up like that?"

"Some are thieves. Some have broken the laws set out by the King. Some are enemies of the King and have plotted against him," Louis said. "Surely you have prisoners in your dungeons in Britain."

"Well, kind of. How long will they have to stay in here?" Lucas said.

"Until their hanging or beheading. Others will stay in the dungeons until their natural death," he answered. "You should beware, *mes amis*. Our King has not been himself of late. He has returned from war very angry. I know you are only hiding from the...bad knight. Just make certain you do not anger the King. You could end up in here, too."

"Don't worry. We don't intend to stay that long," Lucas said.

❦12❧

Louis led them up the stairway to a big, wooden door. It opened to a kitchen. Although it was late at night, the kitchen was very busy. There was a feast in the castle, and servants bustled around, preparing and serving food. Some were cooking, and others were carrying huge platters of food.

Louis pulled them through the door quickly. He then told them to go wait by a pantry cupboard. They were to stay there until Louis came back. If anyone asked, Nicole was to say they were guests of Sir Jean the Fierce and were there for the feast.

Marvin, Nicole, and Lucas waited quietly while Louis went into another room. Almost all the people in the kitchen were yelling at each other in French. Marvin figured that only the wealthy or

those who traveled were able to learn English. He
felt strange standing in the open with people all
around. He kept getting the feeling that they could
be found out at any moment. Luckily, none of the
servants bothered with Lucas, Marvin, and Nicole.

A large wood-burning oven took up the
opposite wall of the kitchen. Long wooden tables
filled the room. Knives, pots, and dishes cluttered
the shelves. Carcasses of meat hung from hooks on
the ceiling.

"I wonder what happened to Mr. LeClair?"
Nicole whispered.

"He's probably hiding out, just like us. I bet he
changed his clothes and is sneaking around. We'll
have to keep an eye out for him," Marvin answered.

"What if he recognizes us?" Nicole asked.

"He won't. Besides, what would he care? If he
tells on us, we will tell on him. He wouldn't want to
get us into trouble. He could be captured as a spy,
too. After all, he comes from the same place we do,"
Lucas said.

Marvin was about to say something when
Louis came back.

"There. Now, let me show you around the
castle," Louis said.

"Oh good, thanks. We need all the help we
can get. We don't know our way around here at
all," Marvin said.

"I can help you. Pray tell, who is the knight
from whom you run?" Louis asked.

Lucas, Marvin, and Nicole looked stunned. No one said a word.

Finally, Marvin spoke. "The Dark Knight," he said. "He wishes to marry Nicole, but she doesn't want to marry someone as evil as he is. We have to hide her."

Nicole looked shocked. "What?"

"It's okay, Nicole," Marvin said through gritted teeth. "Louis understands that sometimes girls are promised in marriage to a man they don't like. He knows that it would be difficult to marry someone who has treated you badly. And running away from someone who wants to marry you is not a punishable crime. We don't want Louis to think we have committed any crimes, do we?" He stared at Nicole a long time, waiting for her to catch on to why he was lying. This way, Marvin knew that they would have an excuse for running from some fake knight, and Louis wouldn't think they had done anything truly wrong. He would show them around but keep them hidden. It would be a great way to have a tour guide. He waited for her to catch on to what he was trying to do.

Finally, she nodded slowly.

"I do understand," said Louis. "And I believe that a young woman should never have to marry against her wishes. Not even to please her parents. I have not heard of the Dark Knight, but I will make sure he does not find you." He smiled at Nicole, and then he looked away quickly.

"How old are you, Louis?" Marvin asked.

"I have fourteen years," Louis answered. "And you?"

"We are all eleven," Lucas answered.

"That is very young to marry. The legal age to marry is twelve, is it not? And both the man and the woman must agree to be married. Things must be very different in Britain," Louis said.

"Um, yes, it is very different where we come from," Nicole answered. She was blushing. "By the way, I was wondering. Um, what is the date today? We have been gone from home so long."

"It is the twenty-third day of June. No, the twenty-fourth day of June, as it is past midnight," Louis said.

"In the year...?" Nicole said. "Hey, Britain is a long way away. I'm just, um, making sure the year hasn't changed."

Louis looked at her strangely. His eyes grew narrow. "In the year 1450."

"Yes, that is what I thought," she said.

Marvin was grinning. He was right about the portal and right about the coin. He just hoped he was right about how to get back.

"Tonight is the feast of Midsummer," said Louis. "If you have never been to France, you must come and see it. On the evening of the twenty-third of June, great bonfires are lit and feasts are held. It is in honor of the birth of St. John the Baptist. The peasants have small feasts and light the bonfires. And here at the castle, the grandest celebrations occur."

"A real medieval feast?" Lucas said. "Great. I love to eat!"

"Medieval? What is the meaning of this word 'medieval'?" Louis asked.

"Oh no, he meant midsummer. Right Lucas?" Marvin said. He shot Lucas an angry look. The word medieval meant Middle Ages. It referred to the time after the fall of the Roman Empire. People thought that that time period was uncivilized, and referred to it as "the nasty time in the middle of two very modern, civilized times," or the Middle Ages. Louis would not know that he lived in the middle of anything.

"Besides, we can't very well eat. We are hiding, remember?" Marvin said.

"Yeah…that's right. Sorry," Lucas said. There was a loud rumble from his stomach. "Sorry, but I'm starved."

"Really? Someone has starved you? You must be extremely hungry, then," Louis said. "Let us go and see the midsummer celebration in the Great Hall. There we can get you some food. I have friends who work in the King's court. You do not need to worry. You will not be noticed in such a large crowd. The Dark Knight will not find you, I will make sure of it."

Lucas looked relieved. Marvin was hungry, too, but he was too excited to think about food. He was in the castle of King Charles VII, about to see a real feast. It was like a dream come true.

Louis led them through the huge kitchen. The leather shoes they wore did not fit properly. Nicole kept tripping over her own feet. Lucas dragged his feet over the wide, wooden floorboards. When they came to another large wooden door, Louis stopped. He listened for a moment. Marvin guessed that he was making sure not to walk into the room in the middle of a speech.

"Wait right here, and I will see if there is a place to seat you," Louis said. He pushed the massive door open, and the loud hum of voices flooded the kitchen.

Marvin, Lucas, and Nicole waited. The cooks and servers stared at them, but they were too busy to bother with the three young strangers.

Louis returned quickly. He led the three friends into a huge room called the Great Hall. Marvin could see why it was called the Great Hall. Large, colorful banners hung on the walls. Gold braided rope held up the tapestry. Some had words and symbols woven onto them. Others showed large coats-of-arms. Candles burned from their holders along the walls. Large torches stood at the ends of tables. A giant chandelier hanging from the middle of the ceiling lit up the room. Marvin was sure it held at least fifty fat candles. Gleaming swords were displayed on the walls. The wooden floor was strewn with straw and sweet grass. The room smelled of grass, food, and fire.

Wooden tables stretched the length of the room, forming long rows. Marvin looked across to the front of the Great Hall. A row of tables was set up on a high platform, facing the room. People were seated at this head table, looking down the rows of other tables. Some sat in large chairs that looked like thrones. Everyone at the head table had a large chair, and their places were set with silver goblets and shining platters.

The people sitting at the long rows of tables had chairs, too. The people closest to the head table had chairs without arms. The farther away from the head table someone sat, the shoddier their chair was. Midway down the room people sat at stools. Those people closer to back of the room simply sat upon benches. At the back of the room were the musicians, servants, and lowest-ranking people, who had to sit on the floor.

Marvin, Lucas, and Nicole stood near the very back of the Great Hall. When they got over their amazement at what they were seeing, they sat down against the back wall with Louis. No one seemed to question their presence. They did not seem to be noticeable.

The servants hurried around the room carrying food. Each time the servants entered with a platter of food, they went to the head table first. Then the food was passed down the rows of tables. The people at the very back ate last.

"They're still eating this late at night?" Nicole asked Louis.

"*Mais oui*, Nicole. The feast lasts all day and often into the next day. Speakers and entertainers perform in between the courses of food," he said, leaning over so she could hear him.

Marvin watched some of the people eating. They seemed to be sharing plates! Others, the people closest to the back of the room, ate their food out of a hollowed-out loaf of bread. The tops of the loaves had been cut off and were given to the people at the head table. Louis told them these bread bowls were called trenchers. People were eating roasted meat, stews, and meat pies out of the trenchers. When they needed a knife, they took it from their belt. The knives were small, but some had tiny jewels on them. People stabbed their food with the knife and ate it right off the tip of the knife. There were no forks at all.

Lucas laughed to himself. He turned to Louis with a confused look on his face. "These people are drinking out of each other's cups," he said. "Look at them. As soon as one guy puts his silver wine glass down, he wipes it off and then the guy beside him uses it. That is disgusting!"

"Disgusting? Surely in Britain you share your drinking vessels," Louis said.

Marvin was afraid that Louis was going to catch on to the fact that they came from much farther away than Britain. "Louis, my friend here does not go to many feasts. He is but a peasant in my father's court," Marvin said.

Louis nodded. He looked at Lucas with pity on his face. Lucas gave Marvin a dirty look.

Lucas leaned over to Marvin. "Look at the dinner knives they all brought along. They look like the knife you described from Mr. LeClair's desk," he whispered. "The people at the front of the room have knives with tiny jewels in the silver handle."

"Yeah, you're right. Man, you have good eyesight," Marvin said. Obviously Mr. LeClair collected more than just coins. But why did he keep valuable collections at school?

The food came out endlessly. Lucas, Marvin, Nicole, and Louis were able to eat at the back of the room until they were stuffed.

At one point, a man at the head table stood up. He was wearing long robes and a tall hat. A large cross hung from a thick chain around his neck. The room fell silent as he began to speak.

"This is the Cardinal. He is the leader of the Church. He will make a speech now," Louis said.

The Cardinal only spoke in French. Marvin couldn't really understand it. When the speech was finished, everyone clapped.

"What did that man say?" Marvin whispered to Louis.

"He said a blessing on the royal family and on the food. Then he thanked the King for changing his mind about the printing invention by Gutenberg," Louis said.

Marvin was surprised. The Cardinal was talking about the Gutenberg Press. They had learned about it in school. It was the first machine that printed books. Before the Gutenberg Press, people had to write out entire books by hand. With no photocopiers or printers, it took forever just to produce one book. That was why books used to be so expensive and so rare. The Gutenberg Press was the invention that changed the way people learned. Books could be printed quickly and cheaply. Peasants gained access to books and information, thanks to that invention.

"What do you mean, *changed his mind?*" Marvin asked.

"A few years ago, King Charles VII was a great supporter of the printed word. He liked to think that books could be made faster and less expensively than the scribes could do them. Now, since he came back from battle, he has changed his mind. The Cardinal and the Pope are happy. The Church does not want any such device to change the way books are made. Scribes are blessed and do great work. The King will not support any such invention any longer. Everyone is happy," Louis said.

"Why? Isn't it better to make more books and make them quickly? Then anyone can learn to read.

Everyone can afford to buy books," Marvin said. He was shocked. *Why would anyone want to put a stop to the invention that changed the course of history?* he wondered to himself.

"No, it is very important that scribes write the books. This wicked printing machine could create nonsense that people will read. Only the nobles and royals should have access to books and learning. Peasants need to work the land," Louis said.

Before Marvin got a chance to say anything, a man came out into the middle of the room. He had three swords with him. Marvin was nervous. It looked a little dangerous to him. The man started tossing the swords in the air. Musicians played little instruments that looked like long flutes and little guitars. The guests cheered and clapped. It was a great party!

Marvin watched the people at the head table closely. He couldn't believe he was looking at King Charles VII himself. From his seat on the floor at the back of the room, Marvin could barely even see him. Still, he thought it was cool, even if the King was at the opposite end of the huge room.

Marvin yawned and wondered what time it was. He looked down at his wrist and gasped. He had left his watch on! He didn't want anyone to see it. He knew that the clock was not invented until 1656—and that was a huge pendulum clock. A small watch would not have been invented until many, many years after that. Something like this could blow their cover and get them labeled as witches. Or worse, it could alter the course of history forever. Marvin quickly checked the time. It was four o'clock in the morning. He unbuckled his watch. He had no pockets in his tights, so he stuffed it in the waist. Then he put his shirt back down over the tights to hide the bulging watch.

⚜13⚜

The feast lasted for hours. When it began to die down, Louis took them for a tour of the castle. They saw the chapel, which was filled with stained-glass windows and little wooden benches. A square altar covered with a red velvet cloth stood at the far end of the room. A large, golden cross was placed on that altar, along with two white candles perched in golden candleholders. Red velvet curtains hung across doorways.

Next, they visited the armory, where pieces of armor and helmets were made and stored. Helmets were perched on shelves and seemed to watch their every move. Metal gloves, called gauntlets, lay near one wall. Marvin thought they looked like claws.

Metal plates of all shapes and sizes hung around the room. Tools and bits of metal lay near a small fireplace. Marvin looked around in complete awe, while Lucas tried to figure out how someone would wear each metal plate. Louis even helped Lucas try on some of the metal armor. When he had a few pieces of armor on, Lucas tried to walk. The armor was so heavy that he could barely even take a step.

Marvin was thrilled with the castle tour. He especially loved the Great Hall and the toilet rooms, called garderobes. These rooms were high up in the castle. They hung out over the castle wall and had a hole in the floor. When someone used the toilet, all the waste fell straight down into the moat below. *No wonder that big pond surrounding the castle stinks*, Marvin thought.

By the afternoon, Lucas, Marvin, and Nicole were exhausted. They hadn't slept all night, and the morning had been busy. Now they had to try to keep out of sight all afternoon until they could leave again at midnight. All three of them were happy when Louis led them back down to the dungeons for a quick nap. The dungeons were dark and cool. They fell asleep close by one another in a corner of an unused jail cell.

They awoke a few hours later, rested and eager to see more of the castle grounds. Louis took them out to the courtyard for the jousting tournament. Hundreds of people took their seats in the courtyard to watch the fight. Peasants stood along the sidelines.

Nicole was upset. She didn't want to see anyone get hurt. "If someone is going to be killed, I'm out of here," she said to Louis.

Louis laughed. "*Non, non.* No one dies at these tournaments hardly ever anymore," he said. "You need not worry. The King simply wants to show the peasants how good his army is. The peasants like to see that their money is going to good use. These knights are from King Charles' court, and some are from Germany. The winners will each be awarded a bag of gold," Louis explained.

"Don't they get hurt?" asked Lucas.

"Not badly," Louis said. "The knights use blunted lances and must only knock their opponent off his horse."

"What is that fence for?" asked Nicole.

"It is not a fence, it is a tilt. The tilt keeps the two knights from running into each other." He pointed to a wooden wall running the length of the field. The knights would ride toward each other on either side of the tilt.

Lucas, Marvin, and Nicole stood in the crowd with Louis, who seemed upset. Louis told them that he wanted to be a part of the preparations. He said that squires were usually at these tournaments with their knights. They would help them suit up into their armor and prepare the weapons. It was part of a squire's training to become a knight. Sometimes, squires got invited to battle. Then they were able to show the King and the other knights that they were ready to become knights themselves. This time, Louis had to miss helping with the jousting tournament because Sir Jean was away. Louis watched the preparations with great interest.

"Louis, why do you want to be a knight so badly?" Nicole asked. "It seems like a dangerous job. And all those metal plates all over a knight's body would be so heavy."

Louis smiled. "Nicole, it is an honor to fight for your king. It has been my path since I was a child. I have been training for many years. One day, I hope to defend my kingdom with honor."

"Did you ever want to be something else? Like a noble or something?" she asked.

"You must know as well as I that we do not choose our own path. It is chosen for us when we are born. If you are a peasant when you are born, a peasant you shall always be. If you are a noble, then so you will be. If a royal, then you will lead a kingdom," Louis explained. "Why do you ask such odd questions?"

Nicole shrugged her shoulders.

As he watched the knights mounting their horses, Marvin thought back to history class. The peasants stayed poor, but the rich got richer. Only the rich could afford books. The more he saw of it, the more the feudal system seemed terrible to him. Then Marvin thought about the King and what he wanted to do. It would be a terrible thing if he were able to put an end to the printing press. Peasants would never be able to learn to read. Only nobles would have access to any information at all. Had he lived in medieval times, Marvin would only be a peasant. He couldn't even imagine what his life would have been like then.

As he watched the knights mounting their horses, Marvin saw the King. He was standing up high on a balcony. The King raised his hand and the crowed quieted down at once. Then he spoke to the crowd.

Marvin couldn't understand what the King was saying, but he had a weird feeling in his stomach. He looked at Nicole and Lucas. They were staring up at the balcony with strange looks on their faces. Something was familiar about that voice. Marvin thought it sounded just like someone he knew.

The knights started to ride up and down the field. Trumpeters played the music that signaled the start of the joust, and colorful flags and banners waved high in the air. Marvin tried to pay attention to the tournament, but he couldn't get rid of the funny feeling in his stomach. He kept looking up at the King. He had to get a closer look at him.

"There is something strange about the King," Marvin said in Nicole's ear. "Did he sound familiar to you?"

"He did for a minute, but I just think I'm homesick," Nicole said.

"Well, I need to take a closer look. I have a funny feeling," he said. He hit Lucas' arm. "Come on," he said loudly. They told Louis that they would be right back. As the crowd cheered and hollered, Marvin, Lucas and Nicole walked over toward the stone balcony. Marvin lifted up the back of his shirt and took his watch out of the waist of his pants. It was eight o'clock. Only four more hours until they would have to go home.

The King had his back to the crowd and was talking to his guards. Each guard was dressed in a red cloak and had a coat-of-arms that read "Scots Archers" sewn to it. Louis had told them that the Scots Archers were the King's bodyguards. Since the 800s, the Kings of France had hired Scottish swordsman and warriors as bodyguards. France greatly trusted the Scottish warriors and also thought it was good to have guards who did not grow up in France. Then they would only have interest in protecting the King. They wouldn't care to get involved in the arguing and struggles of the French court.

Marvin stared at the balcony. The King had his back to the crowd for a long while. Just as Marvin turned to say something to Lucas, Lucas' eyes bugged open. Then his jaw dropped. Nicole had the same look on her face. Marvin turned back to look at the balcony. The King had turned around to watch the tournament, and they could finally see his face clearly.

All three of them quickly ducked down so that they were hidden in the crowd. Marvin's heart almost stopped beating. There on the balcony, dressed in kingly robes, was Mr. LeClair.

"It can't be. That can't be Mr. LeClair. It's impossible," Nicole said.

"What's impossible? We're here, aren't we?" Marvin said.

"Maybe he's just a guy who looks like Mr. LeClair," Lucas added.

"I can't believe it. I thought he would be hiding out, like us," said Marvin. "No. There is no way our teacher is the King of France."

"You're right. This has to be a strange coincidence. What would a medieval king be doing teaching elementary school, anyway?" Nicole said.

"It totally looks like him," Lucas said, shaking his head. "I don't know. Who else could it be?"

"Well, I have to find out for sure," Marvin said. "Tonight. Before we leave."

Nicole was clenching her hands. "This is too weird," she said. "Let's get out of here. I don't want him to see us."

Marvin, Lucas, and Nicole slipped through the crowd and went back to find Louis. Marvin was feeling nervous. Things were getting even stranger than they were before.

When they got back to the spot where they had left Louis, he was gone. They looked everywhere, but they couldn't find him. The knights on the field were riding their large horses up and down the tilt, and the roar from the crowd was deafening. The knights jabbed at one another with their long lances. Marvin, Lucas, and Nicole were about to head back to the castle when they caught sight of Louis. He was out near the field, suiting up in armor. Another young squire was putting on armor, too. It looked like they were preparing to joust.

"Is he allowed to do that? I mean, can squires actually participate in the jousting tournament?" Nicole asked.

"I don't know. I think if they are invited by the King, and another squire challenges them to a joust, they can," said Lucas.

Nicole looked worried. Marvin watched carefully. Both young squires were given lances, and then they mounted their horses and rode onto the field. Just as they were about to fight, the other squire galloped back over to the fence. Marvin was not sure what he was doing. He squinted his eyes. It looked like the other squire was switching his lance! Marvin looked closely at him when he rode back out. The new lance did not have a blunted end. It was pointed! If the squire took a good jab at Louis, Louis would be killed!

The tournament was announced. The two squires, Louis from France and the other from Germany, would joust for honor. That meant they would not win any money; they would only win the honor of knowing that they were the best fighter. The winner would also get a seat at the head table for the upcoming feast at the castle.

Marvin rushed over to Lucas and Nicole. "That other squire just switched his lance. I saw him. That one isn't blunt. He's going to kill Louis!"

"What?" Lucas asked. "Are you sure?"

"Yeah, I'm sure. And no one seems to have noticed. Not even Louis," Marvin said.

"Well, we can't let him do that," Nicole said. She lifted the skirt of her dress off the ground a bit and started to climb the wooden fence that kept back spectators.

"Nic, you can't go out there! You'll get trampled," Lucas yelled.

"But we have to help him," said Nicole. "Do you have a better idea?"

The squires were out on the field, lances raised high in the air. They each put the long handle under their arm. Their hands gripped the middle of the long lance. The gleaming end stuck straight out in front of them. The horses started to gallop toward each other.

✦14✦

Marvin noticed a man standing nearby. He had long dark hair and a mustache. He stood tall and watched the tournament intently. The man had a friendly-looking face. The King's coat-of-arms was sewn on his tunic. He was surrounded by the Scots Archers.

Marvin figured the man was important and decided to take a chance on him. When he pointed him out to Nicole, she agreed. Within seconds she was tugging at his tunic.

"*Pardonnez-moi*," she said loudly.

The man looked down at Nicole and gave her a polite smile.

"I am a friend of Louis Squire, the boy who is jousting now," she said in French.

The man stared at her. "*Oui?*" he answered.

"The other squire switched his lance. It isn't blunted. We saw him do it," she said. "You have to help Louis. He is a squire for Sir Jean the Fierce of King Charles' court."

The man frowned. He said something back to her in French and quickly looked up at the field. Louis had almost knocked the other boy off his horse. The other squire turned his horse around. His lance was held high. He was about to charge on Louis.

Suddenly, the man hopped the guardrail. He raised his arms in the air, but the jousters did not stop. Marvin thought the man would be run over by the horses. Moments later, four other men ran out onto the field and managed to stop the joust. Both squires were led back to the fence and had their lances checked. The German squire's lance was taken away from him. One of the men sniffed the tip of the lance. Two guards pulled him off his horse and dragged him across the field.

Louis removed his helmet. He looked confused. Moments later, he got off his horse, looking terribly disappointed.

Marvin, Lucas, and Nicole ran along the fence to the other side of the field. Louis was gone by the time they got there, but they did find the man who helped them. He said the tip of the other boy's lance was covered in poison.

They looked everywhere for Louis, but they couldn't see him in the crowd. They finally found him near the stables. The man who stopped the joust was talking to him. The three friends ran over to talk to him.

"Are you okay?" Nicole asked.

"I am well. I do not understand why the joust was stopped. I could have won," he answered, his arms outstretched. He shook his head and sighed heavily. "That was my chance to prove my abilities as a knight."

"No, Louis. That other squire was cheating. That sharp end could have killed you. The lance was also poison-tipped," Marvin said.

"He would not have had the chance to use it. I would have defeated him anyway," Louis answered impatiently.

Then the man who stopped the tournament stepped forward and talked to Louis.

"What did he just say?" Marvin asked Nicole.

"He said that Louis has great ability as a knight. But the other squire had one thing in mind. He did not intend to win. He intended to kill him," Nicole said. "He said that the best knights and best squires are often targets. Knights in other courts try to rid a king of his best fighters so they can later attack the castle and be certain to win. Some people think there may be a plot against King Charles. They are aware now that someone is trying to weaken the King's army. The man says he will look into this at once. He also said that Louis is lucky to be alive."

Louis looked down at the ground and nodded. "*C'est vrai. Merci,*" he said. He looked at his new friends. Then he held his hand towards the man. "This is Jacques Coeur. He is an advisor to King Charles. He is also a friend of my father's."

"Hello. Thank you for helping Louis," Nicole said in French.

The man answered her again in French.

Louis smiled. "Thank you. I know I will be ready soon. I am just eager to prove it," he said.

"Well?" Lucas asked impatiently, waiting for the translation.

"He thanked us for noticing what the other squire was up to. Louis may soon be the King's best knight. They don't want to lose him," Nicole answered. "But now Monsieur Coeur has to go. The King has called on him for an important meeting. The King has not been himself since coming back from battle."

Jacques said good-bye and walked toward the tower. The King and his guards were just leaving the jousting tournament.

"Jacques is a good man," Louis said. "He is the only person who truly knows the King well. He oversaw the castle for the year that the King was gone. The King's only family is his wife, and she lives in another part of the castle. Truly, Jacques is his most trusted friend. He is like a brother to the King."

"Where was the King for a whole year?" Lucas asked.

"He was away at the battle of Normandy," Louis answered.

"That's a long time to be gone," Nicole said.

"*Oui*. You well know how long it takes to travel great distances. Although, you did not even have horses with you," Louis said.

"Oh...yes. They were stolen. That's why we stopped at the castle," Marvin answered. Louis nodded his head.

"Louis, we want to get a closer look at the King before we...have to leave," Marvin said.

"The King has a meeting right now. Maybe we could go in and see him," Lucas suggested.

Louis made a face. "I must tell you, that may not be a good idea. You heard Jacques. The King is not himself. He is very angry these days. I would not want him to find us spying on him. Besides, you are not leaving this instant. You will have time to see the King later."

Louis went into the stables to tie up his horse for the night. Marvin, Lucas, and Nicole looked at each other.

"Well, maybe we could just go back to the castle for a bit," Marvin said. He lowered his voice. "I just need to get a better look at the King. If I can see his eyes, I'll know for sure if it's Mr. LeClair."

"What if he sees us?" Nicole asked.

"He won't. Come on, Nic, don't be such a chicken. We came all this way without any horses, after all," Lucas said, smiling.

Nicole shook her head. "Okay, but I really don't want to get caught. If someone catches us snooping around, people will think we're spies," she whispered.

"Don't worry," Marvin said. He took his watch out of his waistband. "It's nine o'clock. We'll just go inside, try to get a good look at him, and then leave." He looked over and saw Louis coming back toward them. "Shhhhhh!" he warned Lucas and Nicole.

"I am finished here," said Louis. "We will go back to the castle. But I must do some chores this evening before I sleep. I will hide you in the dungeons. You can stay there until morning."

"That will be fine," Marvin said. He did not plan to stay in the dungeons all night. He was going to get a look at that King before he left. Even if it was the last thing he ever did.

❧ 15 ❧

When they got back to the castle, they went in the back doorway. Once inside the dark entrance, they closed the heavy wooden door. A set of stairs went up, and one went down. The entrance smelled damp and terrible. Marvin couldn't figure out if the smell was coming from the moat or from inside the castle. The only good smell came from the fireplaces in the adjoining rooms. Marvin loved the smell of burning wood.

"I will show you the way back to the dungeons. You can sleep there until morning. The guard on duty tonight will not bother you. He is always sleeping," Louis said.

Marvin didn't tell him that they were leaving that night. He didn't know how to explain where they were going and how they would get there.

"Where does that stairway lead?" Lucas asked, pointing to the set of stairs on his right.

"Up to the Royal Chambers. The King, the Scots Archers, and the King's advisors live up there. Never go up those stairs," Louis warned.

Louis led the way to the dungeons. Marvin could hear the moans of the prisoners again. The sound gave him the creeps. They walked down the dark stairs. The sound of dripping water echoed from a far corner. The farther into the dungeon they went, the worse the smell got.

The guard at the end of the long, dark hallway was asleep. Louis took them to an empty prison cell and brought in some fresh straw. Lucas, Marvin, and Nicole pretended to settle in for the night. Louis said good-bye and left.

Marvin quietly followed him and listened as Louis went up the stairs. When he heard the door close, he knew that Louis had gone. Then he went back to get Lucas and Nicole. "Come on, you guys. Let's get upstairs. I want to see that King up close."

"But we just told Louis that we would stay here," Nicole said.

"I know, but my fingers were crossed. See?" Marvin pulled his hand from behind his back. His fingers were crossed and he was grinning from ear to ear. "Listen, we only have a few hours. I can't go back wondering if our teacher is actually a king. I'm going up."

"All right. Let's go," Lucas said.

Nicole just shook her head. "Okay, but you heard what kind of mood the King is in. If we get in trouble, I'll blame you."

"If we get in trouble, it won't matter whose fault it is, Nic. We'll have our heads lopped off," Lucas said, laughing. He took a deep breath and shook his head. "I'm kidding. Don't worry about it. As far as they know, we're just a couple of kids from Britain. Remember? Even if we get caught, why would they want to hurt us?"

"Anything is possible," Marvin said. "Let's just be careful, okay?"

They made their way back to the stairs and crept up both flights. When they got to the second floor, they pried open the wooden door slowly. The creak of the door's black iron hinges echoed through the hall. Marvin peered into the hallway. The stone walls were lit up with torches. The hallway was lined with big wooden doors, all of them closed.

They knew the King was having a meeting with Jacques somewhere; they just had to find him. Quietly, they moved down the hallway, listening for people. They didn't hear anyone.

Marvin led Lucas and Nicole up one more flight of stairs, checking all the hallways, before they finally came across an open door. Marvin peeked in and saw a library filled with books. Down the hall, another room was decorated with wall hangings and swords. Woven carpets lay

The Mystery of the Medieval Coin

across the floor. A large wooden table with chairs took up most of the room. Still no King.

At the fourth floor, they finally heard voices. One wooden doorway down the hall was slightly open, and they could hear men talking.

"There they are!" Marvin said. "Let's go."

They tiptoed down the hallway, past closed doors. The voices were growing louder. It sounded like shouting.

Nicole looked concerned. "Uh oh. The King's in a bad mood again," she whispered.

"Don't worry. I just need a closer look. Then we can run back down to the dungeons again and go home," Marvin said.

The voice definitely sounded like Mr. LeClair. As Marvin got closer, he pressed his back against the wall. Slowly, he moved his head around the corner of the doorway to look inside. Nicole and Lucas did the same.

"I don't think it's Mr. LeClair," whispered Marvin. His heart sank.

"No way," Nicole whispered.

"Oh yes it is," Lucas whispered. "Look at the tiny scar on his left cheek."

"Mr. LeClair has a scar?" Marvin asked.

"I'm a details man," Lucas reminded them.

Suddenly the King looked at the doorway. His eyes met Marvin's with the same icy, green stare he gave Marvin at school. Now Marvin was sure it was Mr. LeClair, too. He swallowed hard.

129

"Qui vient la?" the King bellowed.

Within seconds, his bodyguards were pulling out their swords.

"Let's go!" Marvin whispered.

He turned and took off down the hall, with Lucas and Nicole close behind him. Nicole did her best to keep up, but she kept tripping on the hem of her long dress. Marvin glanced back to make sure she was okay and saw that the King's men were right behind them.

Marvin started to panic. He knew that if the guards caught them, they would be thrown in the dungeons. He tried every wooden door they passed. All of them were locked.

Luckily, they were able to outrun the guards. Some of the guards were too big to run quickly. Others had on heavy pieces of armor, which slowed them down.

Finally, Marvin threw open the door of one room. It was as dark as night inside. Lucas and Nicole followed Marvin in. They looked around quickly for an escape. There was nowhere to go and nowhere to hide. They were trapped.

Suddenly, Lucas pointed to the window. "That's our escape!" he whispered.

"Not again!" Marvin groaned. When they had jumped out of the window in Mr. LeClair's classroom, they had only had to drop a few feet to the ground. Now they would have to do it again— but they were four floors up!

"We have no choice. Besides, it worked before," Lucas said. He sounded nervous.

Marvin ran to the open window. The moat was directly below him. It was a long drop down. The murky water that surrounded the castle did not look inviting.

He quickly climbed onto the window ledge. Lucas and Nicole each ran to another window. Marvin gave a terrified look to his friends, plugged his nose, and slid off the ledge. All three of them splashed into the water below.

Guards leaned out the windows, calling to more guards below. Marvin came up for air and almost puked. The smell was terrible. Then he remembered—the toilets! Louis had shown them the toilet room during their tour of the castle. Waste dropped straight down from the toilet hole into the moat. Marvin winced. He hoped no one was using the toilet right now.

Lucas and Nicole popped to the surface right after Marvin. They had the same looks on their faces. Shock and disgust.

No guards jumped down into the dirty water after them. Marvin could hear their heavy armor clanking as they ran down the castle stairs.

The three friends quickly swam to the drawbridge, which went over the moat and connected the land to the castle. Marvin knew that if they went to the shore, they might not get back over the bridge and into the castle. The gates could close, or the drawbridge could be lifted. If they couldn't get in, they wouldn't make it back to the portal on time. They would miss the midnight deadline. Then they would never be able to go back home.

Lucas climbed onto the slope of land under the drawbridge. He pulled Marvin and Nicole up, too. They all hung onto the wooden rafters under the bridge.

Guards started running from the giant door that led into the castle. They shouted orders to one another. Their heavy footsteps thundered loudly over the bridge as they ran to search the land outside the castle.

When the last of the guards had crossed overhead, Lucas pulled himself onto the bridge. He helped Nicole and Marvin up, too.

"You just love all this action hero stuff, don't you? Jumping out of windows and hanging under bridges. This is everything you dream about, isn't it?" Nicole said to Lucas. Her dress was drenched and clung to her legs. She lifted the skirt a bit and tried to wring out some of the water.

"Hey, I knew all that cartoon watching would come in handy some day," Lucas said, grinning.

They started to head back into the castle. They had to find their way back to the dungeons. The problem was, they had no idea how to get there. Marvin was soaking wet and worried.

"Psssst! This way," they heard a voice say from a nearby doorway. The voice did not sound like an angry guard. Marvin wasn't sure if he should trust the voice, but he decided that they had few options.

Marvin stepped into the open doorway. Lucas and Nicole followed. The door closed quickly behind them.

Marvin strained his eyes to see who had saved their necks. It was Louis!

"You do find trouble, *mes amis*, do you not?" Louis asked. "Has the Dark Knight found you?"

"Um, we aren't sure," Nicole said. They glanced at one another but didn't say anything in front of Louis. They really didn't know if Mr. LeClair had recognized them.

"Follow me," Louis said.

They followed Louis down dark corridors. He carried a torch to light the way. It was hard to see anything ahead of them, so they had to go slowly down the stone steps.

Marvin wished he had his trusty flashlight. It was attached to his belt loop on his shorts, which were still hidden in the dungeon. Marvin knew he could not use his flashlight there, anyway. Any modern invention would attract attention. He didn't want to do anything that could disrupt history and change the future.

After a long walk, they were finally in the dungeons again. Marvin never thought he could be so happy to see a dungeon!

"I thought you were going to wait here," Louis said.

"I know. Sorry. We just had to see the King," Marvin said.

"Oh, you are lucky he did not see you. I am told our King just put Jacques Coeur in the dungeon," Louis said. He looked sad. "Who knows what he would do to you."

"I thought Jacques was his most trusted advisor," Lucas said.

"He was. But now the King has accused him of a crime and has sentenced him to prison," Louis said. "It is very bad. Our King is like a different man since coming back from battle."

"You can say that again," Lucas said.

"*Pardon?*" Louis asked.

"Lucas has bad hearing. He needs you to say it again," Marvin said. He shot Lucas a dirty look. Louis believed that they were all from Britain, but if he knew just how far away they really lived, he would surely turn them in.

Louis looked at Lucas with pity. It was the same look he had given Lucas at the feast when he found out that Lucas was a peasant in Marvin's family's kingdom.

"I must go back upstairs. Please stay here and do not get into more danger," Louis said loudly, making sure that Lucas could hear him. "I will return in the morning. We will have to get you to the public bath. You all smell terrible. We really do not recommend that you swim in the moat."

"We figured that one out, thanks," Lucas said.

"Louis," Nicole said. "Thanks for helping us. And thanks for…everything."

"And thank you for helping me at the joust. Now I have friends from Britain," he answered, smiling. "I will see you in the morning. *Bon soir.*"

Marvin felt guilty. They would be long gone by morning. They would probably never see Louis again. Their friend would wonder what had happened to them.

When Louis left, they walked quietly to the hallway where they had first arrived. The stone wall at the end of the hall was lit by torchlight. The carving on the wall looked the same as it did the night before. It was as dark and quiet as ever.

Marvin took his watch out and strapped it onto his arm. He pushed the button, and the watch lit up. It was 11:35 at night. Marvin was so tired that he could barely stand. Except for their short nap that afternoon, they had been awake for more than twenty-four hours.

As they sat on the dirt floor with their backs to the wall, Marvin tried to keep awake. If they fell asleep, they could miss the portal forever. They had to wait just twenty-five more minutes.

Soon, a bigger fear occurred to him.

"Oh no," Marvin whispered. Lucas and Nicole had their heads back against the wall. They looked like they were sleeping.

"What now?" Lucas whispered, cracking one eye open.

"I hope we don't get company," Marvin said.

❧ 16 ❧

Marvin had not thought about it until that very moment. Now it was a real worry. Mr. LeClair would be coming down there any minute. He would have to use the portal by midnight, too.

"Crap," Lucas said. "Okay. We have to be ready the second it becomes midnight. We'll try to go through before him. Hopefully he won't see us."

"If he hasn't seen us already," Marvin said. He checked his watch. 11:45. They sat quietly for ten more minutes. No one seemed to come down to the dungeon—there was no sign of Mr. LeClair.

At 11:55 Marvin got up. "Where's the coin?" he asked. Lucas was the only one who had a modern-day coin made in the year they left.

Lucas' face dropped. "It's in my shorts," he answered, smacking his forehead with the palm of his hand. "Our clothes are still buried in the straw down by that guard."

Marvin got up immediately and crept down the dark hallway.

"Hurry!" Nicole hissed.

Marvin managed to sneak up behind the guard, find their clothes, and get back without the guard even flinching. When he got back to Lucas and Nicole, he fished out the coin. Suddenly, they heard a door open and a man's voice echo through the basement. The man was yelling in French.

"What did he say?" Marvin asked Nicole.

"He's telling someone to hurry up and lock up the prisoner. He wants the guard to go help find the spies. He says he will check on the prisoner himself," Nicole whispered.

Marvin knew it was King Charles—or rather, Mr. LeClair. He was obviously having Jacques thrown into prison. *And then he's going to use the portal*, Marvin thought. *He'll see us for sure!*

He could hear chains rattling. Then the guard's footsteps running up the stairs.

"Let's go!" said Lucas. "He'll be here any minute! We have to be gone before he gets here."

"I can't hurry it up. It'll only work at midnight. Hold onto me like we did last time. Nicole can hold onto your waist. I hope this coin works," Marvin said.

Down the hall, Jacques was pleading to be let free. The King's voice answered angrily. Nicole understood everything. She told the boys that the King said Jacques knew too much and could not be allowed to ruin his plan.

The sound of King Charles' footsteps was getting closer and closer. Lucas stood behind Marvin and held onto him around his waist. Nicole held onto Lucas.

"As soon as we get there, run for the rocks and hide. He'll be right behind us," Marvin whispered.

Marvin's head hurt. He squeezed his eyes shut. The sound of footsteps was getting louder. The King was going to be in that hallway any second. Marvin hoped it would be midnight soon. When his hand started to tingle, he sighed. *Home sweet home*, he thought.

A tiny dot of light appeared on the wall. It swirled and got larger and larger. Soon, it was a glowing circle of light on the wall. Marvin stepped into the spinning circle of light.

A second later they landed on the floor of the cave in the woods. They scrambled for the rocks and hid.

They made it just in time. The wall lit up again and Mr. LeClair, King Charles VII of France, landed on the ground. He got up quickly and left the cave.

Lucas, Marvin, and Nicole waited behind the rocks. They were afraid Mr. LeClair would be waiting for them. After a long while, Marvin crawled out.

"I think he's gone," he whispered. He reached for his flashlight. It wasn't there. He realized that they forgot to change their clothes. All three of them came out from the cave, breathing heavily. They stumbled through the dark forest, hearts pounding. Every crackle, every howl, made their blood run cold. They looked left and right, expecting a surprise attack from a hiding Mr. LeClair, but there was no one in the woods except for them. Finally they made it beyond the trees to the dead-end street. No one said a word.

"Nice tights," Lucas finally said, a dead-serious look on his face.

Marvin looked down at his outfit. Then he looked at Nicole in her long, wet dress. He started to giggle a bit when he looked over at Lucas, with his long tunic and tights. He thought Lucas looked like Peter Pan. For a moment, they stood in the darkness, giggling from nervous laughter. Finally, Marvin shook his head and cleared his throat. They stopped laughing and started walking down the moonlit street.

"Call me," Marvin said as they walked toward his house.

"Yeah, I will," Nicole said.

"Sure, after I sleep for a few days," Lucas said. "And have a really long shower."

Marvin was afraid his parents might be awake. If they caught him sneaking back in, he would not only have to explain where he had been in the middle of the night, but why he was wearing those clothes. Luckily, when he looked up at his house, no lights were on. He checked his watch. It was 12:24. Really, he had only been gone a little while. It was still Monday night. Marvin heaved a sigh of relief, went to the front porch, and climbed the trellis. Then he walked across the roof to his open window and climbed inside.

The first thing Marvin wanted to do when he climbed in the house was take a very long shower. He still stunk from landing in the moat. His mother didn't wake up when he climbed in the window, but she did wake up when she smelled him from down the hall. She also wondered why Marvin was showering so late at night. He said he had thrown up on himself. He smelled bad enough that the excuse worked. His mother let him sleep away the day on Tuesday, which was much different from his usual eight o'clock wake up calls.

Marvin called Lucas and Nicole on Tuesday night. They had both been sleeping all day, too. Luckily, their parents all thought the three friends had caught the flu. None of them had been caught sneaking out.

On Wednesday morning, Marvin was nervous to go to school. He was afraid of seeing Mr. LeClair. He had made a plan with Lucas and

Nicole. They would go to school as though nothing had happened. When they saw Mr. LeClair, they would act normally. After all, he couldn't exactly accuse them of traveling back in time—no one would believe him. If Mr. LeClair did say anything about it, they would just have to deny it and pretend that they didn't know what he was talking about. Hopefully, that would convince Mr. LeClair that he had just seen some other kids who looked like them.

For the one millionth time, Marvin told his mother he felt better. She checked his temperature. Finally she agreed to let him go to school.

Marvin took a deep breath of warm summer air as he left the house. He walked down the street with his backpack on his back. He knew he probably wouldn't need it. It was the last week of school. They weren't going to be doing very much work. Although, Marvin figured, he would have to start cleaning out his locker and his desk. And Lucas', too. Now that was going to be interesting. Lucas kept everything he owned in his locker and his desk.

He met up with Lucas on the way. Lucas looked a bit nervous, too.

"Hey, how's it going?" Lucas asked. He had a baseball hat on backward and was wearing a pair of black sunglasses. His basketball jersey hung down over his long, denim shorts, and he was wearing his favorite running shoes.

"Much better than yesterday," Marvin answered. "I was bagged. I slept all day. I don't know how Mr. LeClair does it. He works all day, and then puts in a full day in France. No wonder he looks so scraggly."

"He gets to sleep in France, you know. It is twenty-four hours. He probably travels there at midnight, goes to bed, and then puts in his full day. Then he travels back at midnight and goes to bed here. Come on. He should be getting plenty of rest. But no wonder he smells so bad. No soap, bathing is rare, and you have to live around the moat. Brutal," Lucas said.

"Next time, we'll have to get some sleep when we arrive. Then we won't be so tired all day," Marvin added. They walked down the quiet street and reached the path by the school.

Lucas stopped dead in his tracks at the end of the path, just before the soccer field. "Hey, who said anything about next time? We almost got caught *this* time. Would you actually go back?" he asked.

"Oh no, I was just thinking…you know…we should have slept," Marvin said. They started walking again and crossed the large soccer field to the school. The schoolyard was swarming with kids. Marvin squinted his eyes to look at the teachers out on yard duty. He hoped Mr. LeClair wouldn't be one of them.

Even though they had barely escaped medieval times, Marvin had loved it. Logically, he knew they should never go back. There was no reason to go back. Besides, they all knew it was too dangerous. The only problem was, it was also the most incredible adventure they had ever been on. It would be hard to let it go. Seeing history up close like that was amazing. Marvin knew he would never, ever forget it.

When they got to the school, Nicole ran up to them. "Whoa, pulling out the basketball shoes now, huh Lucas? To what do we owe this honor? I thought those were your *special, indoor, on-the-court shoes*," Nicole said. She made quotation marks in the air.

Lucas was very particular about his shoes. He had a pair for every sport. His basketball shoes were only supposed to touch the wooden gym floor. He swore he would never wear them outside.

"Ha ha. They are almost worn out, so now they are my outdoor basketball shoes. I'm getting a new special, indoor, on-the-court pair tomorrow. Besides, if Mr. LeClair recognized us the other day in France, I'll need these shoes to run like crazy!" he said, laughing.

Nicole was not laughing. "I know. I'm sick to my stomach. What if he knows it was us?"

"Remember what we said? We act normal. Nothing happened. He will think he saw some other dumb kids. Case closed. Besides, we aren't going to blow his cover. Who would believe us?" Marvin said.

"Yeah, who would we tell, anyway? It's not like we can call up the local gossip column." Lucas put his hand to his ear to make a phone. He spoke into his pinky. "Hello, Moon Reporter Scag Mag? Yes, I have a story for you. I'm in grade five, and my social studies teacher is actually King Charles VII of France. *Mmmmm hmmmm.* Yup. Okay, I will stuff a sock in my mouth and give my head a shake. Thanks," he said in a whiny voice. He pretended to hang up.

Nicole punched him on the arm. "I know we won't tell anyone. But does he know that? We're not dealing with an average guy, you know."

"No, we're dealing with a king. And speaking of the King, why is he here, acting like a teacher? It's not like he needs the money. I mean, come on. I'm sure that castle is worth some bucks," Lucas said.

"I know, I've been thinking about that, too. Why is he spending his time here? Maybe he's trying to bring stuff back to medieval times," Marvin said.

"Maybe he's going to find out all the inventions in the past few hundred years and pretend they are his. He could make tons of money," Lucas said.

"Lucas, he already has tons of money. I mean, he's a king! My question is this: why is he putting a stop to the Gutenberg Press? He is a teacher, and he can see how important books are," Marvin mumbled, thinking hard.

"Well, he sure finds something interesting in modern times. He reads more books than anybody I know. He's finding out all kinds of stuff he shouldn't know about. What if he uses that information back in medieval France? He could change history, you know," Nicole said. "And why is he hanging out here so long? Wouldn't he just come here, find out what life is like, and go back to being a king?"

"You're right, Nic. He's reading a lot of books. He must be looking for something. Something he can use in medieval France," Marvin said. He started getting a bad feeling. King Charles VII was here for a reason. He was obviously looking for something. And the key was in Mr. LeClair's desk.

"Are you thinking what I'm thinking?" Lucas asked. He was grinning widely.

Marvin smiled and nodded. "Yup. We have to go back in," he answered. Lucas raised his right hand. Marvin slapped it. Nicole rolled her eyes.

It was a great day, for a Wednesday. Marvin decided that there was no better week of school than the week before summer break. Report cards were done and over with, teachers were happy and excited, and kids were happy and excited.

When Lucas, Marvin, and Nicole walked into the school, they looked around for Mr. LeClair. The halls were crowded. It was noisier than usual, too. Marvin stretched his neck to look above the heads of the students in the hallway. He could see Mrs. Wright talking to the principal. There was no sign of Mr. LeClair.

"Charlie alert by the library," Lucas said into his hand.

"What?" Nicole asked, looking around.

"Charlie alert. King Charles. Come on, people. Work with me here. Look over by the library," Lucas said, sounding annoyed.

Mr. LeClair was standing outside the library door. Lucas and Marvin had to turn left at the end of the hall to get to their classroom. Nicole had to turn right—she would be walking right past the library. That meant that Nicole had to go past Mr. LeClair.

"Oh no. I can't face him alone!" she complained. "I'll crack! Come on, you guys. Help me out. You have to come with me. I went along with your stupid plans."

Lucas and Marvin looked at each other. They shrugged their shoulders.

"The lady does have a point. If he questions her, she'll blow our cover. Rat us out. Squawk like a jail bird…" Lucas trailed off.

"Yeah, I get the point," Marvin said. He shook his head. They were supposed to be avoiding Mr. LeClair. Now they were walking straight into danger. He took a deep breath. "Let's go," he said.

They all turned right and headed down the hall toward Nicole's classroom. They passed Mr. LeClair's classroom and were only a few feet from the library.

Lucas walked ahead and stopped right in front of Mr. LeClair. "Good morning, sir. Nice day, isn't it?"

Mr. LeClair slowly turned his head to face Lucas. He gave him his usual cold stare. "Good morning," he answered. "Yes, it is a very nice day. And how are my favorite students?" he asked with a malicious grin.

"Uh, we're fine, thanks," Nicole answered.

"We wanted to ask you…um…do we need to bring our books to class today? I mean, it's almost the end of the year and all. Maybe we won't need them," Marvin said. He knew it was a dumb question, but it was all he could think of.

Mr. LeClair was acting strange, but he always acted strange. Marvin stared at his face. He was trying to see if Mr. LeClair looked angry or suspicious or anything. If he did recognize them, he wasn't giving it away.

"Of course, Marvin. You must bring your books. School is not out until Friday," he answered in a calm voice. His icy stare told them nothing.

"O...kay. Well. See ya!" Lucas said. He elbowed Marvin and started walking toward Nicole's classroom. When they were farther down the hall, Lucas looked back over his shoulder. "See? He didn't know it was us!"

"Unless he was faking it," Nicole said. "So we don't know it was *him* back there."

"Oh, the old *two-can-play-at-this-game*. So we're pretending it wasn't us back in the castle, and he's pretending it wasn't him?" Lucas asked.

"Maybe," Marvin mumbled. He looked back down the hall toward Mr. LeClair. Mr. LeClair looked back at him and waved. "I'm getting out of here."

"Please, just tell me he doesn't know. I'm going to be sick," Nicole said.

"Okay, he doesn't know," Marvin said.

Nicole sighed. She said good-bye and walked into her classroom. Lucas and Marvin turned around to go back down the hall. Mr. LeClair had gone into his classroom. When they passed the room, he was reading a book again. This time he was laughing to himself.

"That is one weird dude," Lucas said.

Marvin could hardly concentrate all morning. They spent the first part of class doing math. Then they started cleaning out their desks. The whole time, Marvin tried to come up with a plan to get back into Mr. LeClair's classroom. A loud crackle over the intercom got his attention.

Attention teachers. Please be reminded that we have a staff meeting at noon. Everyone must attend.

Then the intercom clicked off. Marvin knew there was a message in that announcement. *Everyone must attend.* That was meant for Mr. LeClair. He skipped staff meetings all the time. Marvin had heard the principal talking about it to the secretary months ago.

"That's our break!" Marvin whispered to Lucas. "The staff meeting! The staff room door will be closed, and we can just go in his classroom. Piece of cake!"

Lucas shrugged. "Okay. Why not? We're already almost busted. Let's go all the way."

At lunchtime, everyone ran to their lockers. Most of the students grabbed their lunch bags and took off for the lunchroom or the playground. Lucas and Marvin stayed behind. A minute later, they heard the principal walking down the hall with Mr. LeClair, who was insisting that he was too busy to come to the meeting. The principal would not take "no" for an answer.

When the coast was clear, Marvin and Lucas slipped out the door and down the empty hall. A second later, Nicole showed up, too.

"Look who got up the nerve to join the spy mission," Lucas said.

"I had to know what was happening," Nicole whispered.

They walked up to Mr. LeClair's messy desk. Books were scattered all over the place.

"He must be looking for something," Marvin said. "Check if any of these books are about buried treasures or anything."

They started flipping through all the books. Nicole sat down on the floor with a history book and flipped to a section about King Charles VII. Marvin wondered why the King would want to read about himself.

They looked all over his desk. There was nothing about an invention he could steal. Nothing but a book on the Gutenberg Press. They already knew he wasn't going to steal that. He actually wanted to destroy it. They found nothing about a treasure. Nothing about money, or coins, or valuables at all. They were almost sure they weren't going to find anything.

"Wait a minute," Nicole whispered. "Do you remember when Louis told us that King Charles VII just came back from battle?"

"Yeah, why?" Marvin asked.

"Because it says here in this book that King Charles VII is supposed to be away at the battle of Normandy right now. He left in 1449. He went to battle in Formigny, then in Caen, and finally in Cherbourg."

"So what?" Lucas asked.

"So, the battle in Cherbourg ended in August of 1450," she answered. She was staring at them. Her face was serious.

"But when we went back in time it was only the end of June 1450. King Charles VII would not be back from battle yet," Marvin whispered.

"Then who is the King we saw the other day?" Lucas asked.

"An imposter!" Marvin said coldly. "Let's get out of here."

❧18❧

After school, Lucas, Marvin, and Nicole went straight to the city library. They wanted to do some research to find out why Mr. LeClair was pretending to be King Charles VII. They also wanted to know who he really was.

They piled their backpacks onto a desk in the brightly lit library. A man behind the desk asked them if they needed any help. They said no and went for the computer. Marvin looked up medieval history and wrote down some numbers, and then they walked over to the other end of the library. They sat down in an aisle between the stacks of books, pulling them one at a time off the shelf.

"Here's the one you were reading in his classroom, Nic," Lucas said, cracking open the book. Marvin moved over to read it at the same time.

"Yup, the real King is gone, all right. LeClair is not the real King," Marvin said.

"Then what is he doing there? And why doesn't anyone know he isn't the real King Charles VII?" Nicole asked.

Marvin was reading further ahead. He flipped the page before Lucas was finished.

"Hey! A little respect, if you don't mind," Lucas complained.

Marvin didn't answer. He was busy reading. Suddenly his eyes popped open. "Well, well, well. Look at this. It says here that some of the King's guards, the Scots Archers, actually looked like the King. They were used as doubles, just in case the King was in danger," Marvin said. "It also gives the exact day King Charles VII returns from battle."

"So?" Lucas said.

"So maybe Mr. LeClair is actually a Scots Archer. Maybe he is planning on using this information about the battle to replace the King," Marvin said.

"What do you mean?" Nicole asked. Her eyebrows were scrunched up and she was biting her nails.

"Well, if he is a bodyguard who looks like the King, then no one would know the difference, right? Besides, the King has been gone for a year. Who would remember exactly what he looks like? The peasants in his kingdom have never seen him up close anyway. What if this imposter king is using the information from these books to get rid of the real king?" Marvin said quietly.

"Like, you mean, kill him?" Lucas asked. He looked worried now.

"Who knows? Mr. LeClair has all the information right here. Where King Charles VII went, when he'll be back, and even what route he took to come back. What if our bodyguard friend plans to meet the real king when he is coming back from battle and kill him? That way, the bodyguard could pretend to be the real king and no one would even know," Marvin said.

"That's brutal. So Mr. LeClair isn't a king at all. He's an imposter king planning on killing the real king. But why?" Lucas asked.

"Who knows. But if he gets away with it, it will change history forever," Marvin added. "Remember what he said about the printing press? These books all around us would not exist. If he kills King Charles VII, history will be changed. *We* might not exist. Even if we *did* still exist, we would probably be peasants." Marvin closed the book.

"No wonder everybody said he was acting strange since coming back from battle. He isn't the King at all. And no wonder he locked up Jacques Coeur. Jacques was the King's closest advisor. He would be able to tell that this King Charles is not the real King Charles. Didn't Mr. LeClair say Jacques knew too much?" Nicole asked. "So now what?" She looked like she knew the answer.

"Well, if you want to save the King and save the course of history, there is only one thing to do," Marvin answered.

Lucas and Nicole nodded their heads. They all knew what had to be done. Someone had to save the real King Charles VII. Someone had to save history. They would have to go back.

And hopefully, they would be able to return home again.

Watch for A.D. Fast's exciting sequel to

The Mystery of the Medieval Coin

www.tealeafpress.com

Special Thanks

Many thanks to Paul Lewis, Susan Roberts, Kate
Johnston and the many readers who helped to shape
this book. Sincere thanks to my partners, the best
editors in the world: Jane Lewis, Heather Evoy, Kate
Calder, and Hannelore Sotzek.

Thanks also to Ben Kooter and Vanwell Publishing.

Extra special thanks, as always, to Ron Fast, and
Luke & Max Fast.